"I'll See Your Ten And Raise You, Um, This Whole Stack Of Money," Audrey Said Triumphantly.

"I don't have any money left," Mark said.

"Well, I guess you could bet something besides money."

"Like what?"

Audrey stopped smiling and looked directly into Mark's brooding blue eyes. "If I win…you stop drinking," she said, "and you shave that awful beard!"

"What the hell kind of bet is that?"

"If you don't think you can do it—"

"Okay, Ms. High-Stakes Player, let's say we up the ante."

"What do you mean?"

It was Mark's turn to look smug as he clasped his hands behind his head. "I'll see your bet by shaving my beard and I raise it by getting off the booze. Now, see my raise by wagering something *I* want, or fold."

Surely he didn't want…. "Um, what do you have in mind?"

His smoldering gaze slid down her body. "I think you know exactly what *I* want. Now, do you fold, or play?"

Dear Reader,

Welcome to another scintillating month of passionate reads. Silhouette Desire has a fabulous lineup of books, beginning with *Society-Page Seduction* by Maureen Child, the newest title in DYNASTIES: THE ASHTONS. You'll love the surprises this dynamic family has in store for you...and each other. And welcome back *New York Times* bestselling author Joan Hohl, who returns to Desire with the long-awaited *A Man Apart,* the story of Mitch Grainger—a man we guarantee won't be alone for long!

The wonderful Dixie Browning concludes her DIVAS WHO DISH series with the highly provocative *Her Fifth Husband?* (Don't you want to know what happened to grooms one through four?) Cait London is back with another title in her HEARTBREAKERS series, with *Total Package.* The wonderful Anna DePalo gives us an alpha male to die for, in *Under the Tycoon's Protection.* And finally, we're proud to introduce author Juliet Burns as she makes her publishing debut with *High-Stakes Passion.*

Here's hoping you enjoy all that Silhouette Desire has to offer you...this month and all the months to come!

Best,

Melissa Jeglinski

Melissa Jeglinski
Senior Editor
Silhouette Desire

Please address questions and book requests to:
Silhouette Reader Service
U.S.: 3010 Walden Ave., P.O. Box 1325, Buffalo, NY 14269
Canadian: P.O. Box 609, Fort Erie, Ont. L2A 5X3

High-Stakes Passion

JULIET BURNS

Published by Silhouette Books

America's Publisher of Contemporary Romance

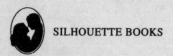 **SILHOUETTE BOOKS**

ISBN 0-373-76644-0

HIGH-STAKES PASSION

Visit Silhouette Books at www.eHarlequin.com

Printed in U.S.A.

Books by Juliet Burns

Silhouette Desire

High-Stakes Passion #1644

JULIET BURNS,

having had the good luck to be born in Texas, can't imagine living anywhere else. She's lucky to share her life with a supportive husband, three rambunctious children and a sweet golden retriever. She likes to think her emotional nature—sometimes referred to as *moodiness* by those closest to her—has found the perfect outlet in writing passionate stories late at night after the house gets quiet. She's inspired by the three C's: country music, cowboys and chocolate. Juliet loves reading romance novels and believes they have the power to change lives with their eternal message of love and hope. She'd love to hear from readers. You can contact her by visiting her Web site www.julietburns.com.

For my patient hubby, who gave up home-cooked meals, for my best CP, Pam, who read this book as much as I, and for Mama, who watched my kids so I could write.

One

"**I**'ve missed you, darlin'," a deep voice mumbled as a large, masculine body pressed against Audrey's back.

She yelped and tried to move, but his hand stole around her waist. His warm lips nuzzled her neck and sent a tingle down her spine. Audrey was too stunned to move.

The man grabbed her shoulders and spun her around. "I need you tonight, baby." The man's words were slurred, and the smell of beer wafted from his breath, but the yearning in his voice kept her from reacting. He lowered his mouth to hers and captured her lips in a deep and thorough kiss.

His firm mouth moved over hers and he pulled her closer. When his hand slid down to squeeze her bottom, she snapped out of her haze. In one swift move she pulled her lips from his, shoved against his chest and kicked his shin.

She grabbed a knife from the block on the counter behind her as he stumbled backward. She was alone in a strange house. The only person who knew she was here was her editor.

"Damn, woman!" the man bellowed as he leaned against the kitchen island. He grasped his right leg with both hands. Long hair covered half his face, but she saw his eyes squeeze shut and his face twist in a grimace of pain.

"Jeez, you didn't have to do that." His jeans and flannel shirt were rumpled, and his jaw was covered in heavy stubble. Maybe she should rethink this posing-as-a-housekeeper idea. Surely there was a safer way to earn a promotion to staff writer.

Her hands trembled. "You—you grabbed me." Her voice shook and she couldn't catch a breath. This couldn't be the famous rodeo champion she'd come here to interview.

His eyes opened wide and his brows rose. He scowled at the knife. "Put that thing down. I'm not gonna hurt you."

With a jolt of disbelief, she recognized his beautiful blue eyes. Her stomach pitched. It couldn't be.

Mark Malone. *The Lone Cowboy.*

The reclusive cowboy had been thrown from a bull in Cheyenne five months ago. The last anyone had seen of Mark Malone, he was being carried out of the rodeo arena on a stretcher. His press agent had since refused all interviews. Audrey had pictured him in a wheelchair, or worse.

"You're him! I mean…it's you."

"I'm who?" Mark rubbed his aching shin as the woman dropped the knife to the floor. Not that she'd needed any weapon besides her lethal kick. She sure as hell wasn't Jo Beth. He should've known Jo wouldn't show up out here.

After the accident, she'd moved on to the next rodeo star. He hobbled to a chair, pulled it out and dropped into it.

"You're the *Lone Cowboy.*"

He sneered. "Not anymore." Mark took in the woman's stained, baggy sweats and disheveled hair. How the hell had she gotten in? Was she a crazy fan? A reporter? Who else would show up at his ranch uninvited? "Who are you?"

Her brows rose and she pointed at herself. "I'm the new housekeeper." The last word rose to a higher octave, as if she were asking him.

"Housekeeper? My foreman never mentioned anything about another housekeeper." He peered at her more closely, taking in the figure her sweatshirt couldn't disguise. Too young, too...

"Maybe you were too drunk to remember the conversation!" She gasped, and clamped both hands over her mouth, eyes widening.

Too interfering! Mark glared through narrowed lids. She was accusing him of being a drunk? Hell, after the news the doctor had given him today, he'd had cause for a few longnecks. "Even if he did hire you, you're fired. I don't want you here." If he was going to live with pain the rest of his life, he wanted to get drunk in peace.

Her eyes enlarged even further. She stooped to retrieve the knife and turned her back to him, dropping it in the sink with a clatter. "John *did* hire me. You can confirm my employment with him. I'm sorry if I hurt you, but—"

"If? Lady, you damn near—" He'd been about to say she'd crippled him. But he was already a cripple. "You're a menace! Just go back to wherever you came from. I don't need a housekeeper."

She rounded on him, hands propped on her curvy hips.

"You need more than a housekeeper. You need a miracle!" The spitfire brushed past him and stomped out of the kitchen.

That took care of that. The last thing he wanted was some busybody snooping around. He grabbed a bottle of whiskey, headed for the den and slumped in his recliner. Might as well finish what he'd started. His damn leg was killing him.

A half hour later, the whiskey had done its work. Feeling no pain, Mark was half watching some late-night talk show. Out of the dark, someone yanked the remote from his hand.

He looked up as John turned off the TV. "The new housekeeper just called. Said you fired her."

"I don't want her here. She's too…snippety." John was more than his foreman. He was the closest thing Mark had to a father.

John sighed. "Mark, when was the last time you ate something decent?"

Mark leaned up and grabbed the remote, snapping the TV back on. "I'm fine."

"Well, I'm not! I can't stand to see you this way!"

Jaw clenched, Mark stared at the television.

John moved between him and the big screen, folding his arms over his chest. "Look, son. I tried being patient. I know life's dealt you some lousy hands. But you never let it beat you before. You gotta cowboy up."

"Let it go, John," Mark said through gritted teeth. The only thing he'd ever been good at, the only thing that made him forget who he really was, had ended. He just wanted to be left the hell alone.

Shaking his head, John cursed under his breath, something Mark had rarely heard him do. "Have it your way. Hide from the world. But if you want me to stay on, the housekeeper stays, too. We've already had two quit, and you need this place cleaned up if you want to sell. We're lucky this one even walked past the front hall." John stared at him a minute, threw up his hands and headed for the door.

Mark scowled. Would John really quit? Mark did want to unload this parcel of pipe dreams. He supposed for two weeks, just until roundup was over…

"John," he called after him. When the foreman turned around, Mark forced himself to meet the look of disappointment in his eyes. "All right. She can stay."

After John called her back, Audrey shed her clothes and fell into bed, only to stare at the ceiling. She'd spent all day scrubbing the kitchen, and every muscle in her body ached. But that's not what kept her awake.

All the fantasies she'd had of her hero had met a quick, painful death. If she hadn't been so desperate to get this story, she'd have turned around and headed back to Dallas.

Disillusionment tightened her throat. She'd arrived at the *Lone Cowboy's* ranch this morning envisioning romantic western decor, but the house had looked more like the scene of a barroom brawl. The odor of stale food, flat beer and cigarette smoke permeated the rooms. The kitchen table had been covered with fast-food trash, overflowing ashtrays and empty beer bottles.

She took a deep breath, turned and bunched her pillow. She couldn't believe that disheveled drunk was the same hero who'd rescued her all those years ago. Closing her eyes, she remembered the night she'd first met him.

She'd been curled up in his stallion's stall to write her article for the school paper…

"Hey, fatso! Aren't you in the wrong building? The hogs are over there!" Raucous laughter followed the taunt.

Audrey flinched and broke the tip off her pencil. Oh, God. Not again. It was the same pack of teenage boys who'd harassed her at the concession stand. She squared her shoulders and stood to face them.

The bullies advanced, making snorting noises.

Audrey clutched her notebook to her chest, forcing herself to hold her ground. "Get lost, losers!"

The leader's eyes flashed and he advanced on her.

"What are y'all doing in here?" a deep voice bellowed from the stall's doorway.

The boys spun around to face a tall, broad-shouldered man.

She caught her breath. It was him. Mark Malone.

His white, long-sleeved western shirt stretched across a strong chest and broad shoulders that only emphasized his slim hips. Leather chaps hugged his long, muscular thighs and drew attention to the very male area covered only by his blue jeans.

Audrey was mesmerized.

"None of your business, man," the boy in the middle retorted.

Mark Malone's gaze traveled past the group of boys, landed on Audrey for a moment, then shot to the one who'd spoken. His eyes narrowed and his jaw clenched.

In a split second he reached out, grabbed the boy's shirtfront and yanked him up, nose to nose. He spoke through clenched teeth. "I make my living riding bulls. You know what that means?"

The boy's eyes bugged out and he shook his head frantically, choking on the tight grip around his throat.

"That means I don't care whether I live or die." Mark punctuated the sentence by jerking on the boy's shirt. "I'll take you out back right now and whip all five of your butts

without a second thought." Mark dropped the ringleader and he stumbled back, glaring, but silent. The boys exchanged glances and scrambled away.

The scent of soap and subtle, musky cologne followed him as he approached. "Are you all right?" he asked gently. His black Stetson shaded a strong, square jaw covered with five-o'clock shadow.

Her breathing hitched as she looked up into his deep blue eyes.

He swiped off his hat, revealing chestnut hair that curled just above his collar. Her stomach did a strange flip-flop. He held out his hand, beckoning her as he had in her dreams. "It's okay, they're gone now."

She'd learned to accept her plain face and pudgy body a long time ago, but right now she desperately wished she were beautiful and thin like her sisters. A familiar dull ache settled in her chest.

When she gathered her wits and took his large, callused hand, electric currents shot up her arm.

"Come on, I'll walk you back to the Coliseum." The Fort Worth skyline twinkled behind him as they headed for the arena. "How old are you?"

"Sixteen." Way too young for the twenty-year-old rising rodeo star. Audrey looked at the dusty ground and swallowed. "Thank you for what you did back there."

When he didn't answer, she glanced back up at him. The expression in his eyes was old and weary. "That's what us heroes are for, right?"

She stopped and frowned at his sarcastic tone.

Mark brought his hand up to squeeze her arm and kept it there. The heat from his touch raised the hairs on the back of her neck. "Come on, let's get you back."

A shrill voice called from a few feet away, "Mark! It's

getting late, sweetie, and you promised to take me to Billy Bob's."

He dropped his hand from Audrey's arm and glanced behind him at a beautiful brunette. He looked back at Audrey, shrugged and took her hand, giving it a gentle squeeze. "You'll be all right now?"

At her nod, he pressed her hand once more, flashed a dazzling smile, turned and sauntered off.

This time, the ending changed. Mark came back, scooped her up in his arms and took her mouth in a deep, passionate kiss.

Audrey raised her arms to draw him closer, but an annoying beeping interrupted her, snatching her out of the sensuous dream. She rolled over to turn off the alarm. Four o'clock. She groaned. Time to start breakfast.

Mark woke up sometime close to dawn, stiff from sleeping in the recliner. Damn it! His calf muscle cramped, and he reached down to knead his right leg. He stumbled down the hall to the bathroom in search of aspirin. Flipping on the light caused spears of pain to shoot through his eyelids. He splashed water on his face, ran his hands through his hair and grimaced at his reflection in the mirror. Water dripped off his beard, and his eyes were so red they looked like miniature road maps.

Easy to see why that woman hadn't recognized the *Lone Cowboy*. Guess he had let himself go the last couple of weeks. No wonder John was disgusted. Hell, he disgusted himself.

Mark swallowed the aspirin and left the bathroom. He flopped on the bed, squinting at the daylight filtering through the blinds. A vague memory of luscious lips, a plump, rounded breast and a clean, citrus smell invaded his mind. He'd never get back to sleep now. He was too restless.

Aw, hell. Had he really groped that poor woman last night? What an ass he'd made of himself. He'd clean up, go find her and then apologize. Rolling over to sit up, he groaned and grabbed his head.

Apologies could wait until the aspirin kicked in.

Audrey descended the stairs carefully, exhausted. As she entered the kitchen, the memory of Mark's kiss washed over her. Even drunk, he'd taken her breath away. The memory of his hard body pressing against her sent a wave of desire through her. Mark Malone certainly hadn't seemed injured.

She shook herself back to reality and set an industrial-size pot of coffee on to brew. Frying sausage in a skillet, she concentrated on her mission. Why had he been drinking last night? She'd never heard of him being a wild party animal. Even in his younger days, he'd had a squeaky-clean image. Several early interviews had told of how he used his personal jet to fly foster children to the national rodeo finals, and made a home on his ranch for retired broncs and bulls.

She kneaded the dough for biscuits and popped them in the oven, then opened the refrigerator. A case of beer sat front and center. She shoved it aside and reached for the carton of eggs. At twenty-nine, he'd had a long career for a bull rider. He could have retired even without the accident. What kind of injuries had he sustained?

She needed to investigate further. And she could start by questioning his employees at breakfast.

"Howdy." An older man with a large, crooked nose stood at the back door. He stuck out his right hand as he removed his hat and carefully scraped his boots on the mud catcher next to the threshold. "Welcome to the Double M. I'm John Walsh, the foreman." He cleared his throat. "Spoke with you last night, I believe?"

"Yes. Good morning." Audrey glanced past him to the men gathered on the porch behind him. "Come in and have a seat. Breakfast is almost ready."

John raised his brows and grinned. Then he hitched up the jeans on his lanky frame and stepped into the kitchen.

Audrey busily scrambled eggs and pulled the biscuits from the oven as the hands filed in. John cleared his throat and motioned to the mud catcher. The men stopped and dutifully scraped their boots before entering, and placed their hats on pegs by the door.

"Let me introduce you." John gestured to the dozen men standing around the table. "Boys, this here's Ms. Audrey Tyson." He pointed to the man beside him. "Ms. Tyson, this here's Jim. You watch yourself around him or he'll pour hot sauce in your pancake batter."

"Mornin', ma'am." Jim gave her a two-finger salute.

Next came Dalt. Whoa. Blond hair, chocolate-brown eyes and dimples. He took her hand in both of his and brought it to his lips. "Very nice to make your acquaintance, Miss Audrey." He spoke with a seductive southern drawl.

"Down, boy!" John barked. "You can charm the lady on your own time."

As the introductions continued, Audrey realized that "boys" wasn't quite an accurate description. Ruth was almost six feet tall, her short, dark curls cut stylishly. She wore makeup, but still looked tough enough to more than pull her weight.

Not a Lefty, Shorty or Slim among them, Audrey thought as the rest were introduced. Just a nice bunch of people who happened to be cow-"boys."

But no Mark Malone this morning.

Audrey placed sausage, eggs, biscuits and gravy onto the long kitchen table as a beautiful Border collie trotted up to her, tail wagging and tongue hanging out.

"Curley!" John admonished the dog. "Get out of the kitchen, boy."

Curley? Guess there was a clichéd cowboy name after all. The black-and-white cow dog leaned against her legs. Audrey hunkered down and whispered, "Don't worry, Curley. I'll save a bite of breakfast for ya."

They all took their seats around the table, and Audrey dodged elbows and filled up coffee mugs. She decided to plunge right in. "So, what's it like working for the famous *Lone Cowboy?*"

An unnatural silence enveloped the kitchen.

Their mouths are full. Just give them a minute.

A minute dragged by. Two. No one looked up.

Okay… Maybe good reporters eased into their questions. "He had quite a career, huh? The Professional Bull Riding Association wants to put him in their Hall of Fame. World championship titles in bareback, saddle bronc and bull riding. And he didn't even start riding bulls until after he graduated high school."

Jim looked at her. "You a rodeo fan?"

Audrey nodded. "My dad was world champion saddle bronc, 1973."

"Really? What's his name?" Dalt asked.

Now she was getting somewhere. This wasn't so difficult. "Ever heard of Glenn Tyson?"

"No," Dalt grinned. "Just wanted to know if Tyson was

your maiden name. Didn't see a wedding ring, but you never can tell. You attached, honey?"

Dalt was coming on to *her?* He must be desperate for female company out here in the boonies. Even on a good day, her looks had never inspired flirting. How to steer the subject back to Mark? "Actually, I'm saving myself for the *Lone Cowboy.* He's not married, is he?" Oh my Lord, had she really said that?

Jim spewed his coffee, and the other hands guffawed and snickered.

Ruth looked at her as if she'd just suggested marrying Hannibal Lecter, her mouth open and her eyebrows raised. "Audrey, honey. Don't waste your time," she warned.

"What do you mean? Has he got a girlfriend?"

Ruth shook her head. "I've been working on the Double M a long time, and Mark's never had a relationship last longer than a few months. He dates 'em, but he don't trust 'em."

"But you're a woman," Audrey reasoned, thrilled she was finally getting some information.

"Yeah, but I'm not interested in his heart, girl. Just his cows." Ruth smiled and stood. "Speaking of which, I think it's time we got to it."

Audrey's smile faded. *I'm not after his heart, either.* Just his life story. She swiveled around and headed for the stove, grabbing the pack lunches she'd made earlier for the men, uh, hands.

Taking the sacks, they filed out the door, crammed them into their saddlebags, mounted and rode off. She waved to them from the back porch, rubbing her arms in the brisk morning air. What had possessed her to think she could do this?

Desperation, that's what.

For two years, she'd bided her time at the magazine, passively waiting to be given a chance. Well, no more! The new Audrey went after what she wanted. She raised her chin and straightened her shoulders, remembering her determination to change her life. She'd sat alone on her twenty-fifth birthday, taken assessment of her stagnant existence and vowed to make some changes.

Tonight at dinner, she'd be more discreet. If she just gave it a little time, the ranch hands might open up more. She had a gut feeling the reclusive rodeo champion was a very complicated man. But if she was to make her story work, she needed to figure out the reasons for his behavior. Maybe he had a history of substance abuse, or violent tempers or marathon orgies.

Though it would make a great story, she really hoped there was nothing like that in his past. Her shining hero was already tarnished around the edges. She'd hate for him to fall off his pedestal completely.

After finishing a seemingly endless stack of breakfast dishes, Audrey decided to take a quick break before tackling the dining room. She poured herself a glass of iced tea and stepped out to the covered back porch. Inhaling the fresh, pine-scented air, she listened to a mockingbird's calls and the wind rustling through the trees. She gazed longingly at a cushioned glider and tried not to think about *him.*

Eyes closed, she sipped her tea. *East Texas is so peaceful.* No smog, no traffic. Maybe living away from the city wouldn't be so bad. And she was only thirty miles from Tyler if she got desperate for a mall or a movie theater.

Listen to yourself. You're only here for two weeks.

Her mind registered a sound coming from the kitchen. She opened the screen door to check it out, and stifled a gasp. Mark stood in the middle of the kitchen, all six feet three inches of him, looking impatient and bewildered. Even so, he was impressive.

His hair was still wet from a shower, and his faded jeans and plaid flannel shirt were clean. He still hadn't shaved, but man, was he sexy. He radiated an overwhelming masculine energy that sent waves of excitement coursing through her. But his eyes—she hated to see them so bloodshot, so full of pain.

Somehow, she summoned a confident smile. "Good morning!"

The first thing Mark saw was the bright morning sun shining on her long, dark blond hair. The slanted light reflected off her crown, giving the illusion of a halo. Was this the same woman from last night? Her full lips curved up in a sensual smile. How long had it been since a woman had smiled at him like that? And there was respect and genuine interest in her beautiful green eyes.

Even after last night.

Mark felt gut-punched…and a stirring of interest south of his buckle. "I wanted to apologize." He cleared his throat. "For last night. I thought you were someone else."

Her smile vanished, and she bit one side of her bottom lip. "I'm sorry about kicking—"

"Forget it. I deserved it."

She licked her full lips and crossed her arms, emphasizing her ample curves. Did she realize what that did to a man?

His new housekeeper was not a great beauty. She had a plain, square-shaped face. But her lips were full and sensuous, and her bright green eyes flashed with intensity. She was short, but voluptuous. The loose-fitting T-shirt couldn't conceal the outline of her full breasts.

He'd always preferred a woman that wasn't all skin and

bones. Here was a woman a man could roll beneath him and not worry he might crush her to death. That thought sparked a vision of his hands filled to overflowing, cupping and squeezing those large, perfectly shaped breasts as he rubbed his face between them.

Damn! He was as hard as the titanium pin in his leg. This was just a sign of how pathetically long it had been since he'd had a woman.

"What? Did I spill gravy on myself?" she snapped. Now her eyes sparkled with indignation.

"Huh? Oh, uh…" *Get yourself together, Malone. Take a deep breath and stop staring at her chest.* "Is there any breakfast left?"

"Oh! Yeah." She frowned, avoiding his gaze, and pushed her hair behind her ears. "I made plenty. Let me get—"

"I can get it myself."

She ignored him and went flying past, pulling plastic containers from the fridge and heating a plate of biscuits, sausage and gravy.

"There aren't any scrambled eggs left, but I can whip some up real quick. Maybe I should make a few more biscuits, too." She began pulling out a skillet, eggs and butter, unloading more food than any one man could eat.

He took a deep breath, inhaling the aroma of homemade biscuits. They sure smelled good! He couldn't remember his last decent meal. He grabbed a chair and sat, studying his new housekeeper. She'd walloped him good last night. He almost smiled.

"Was your leg injured in the fall?"

Mark focused his gaze and realized she was standing before him, staring at his right leg with a worried frown. Damn, he'd been absentmindedly rubbing it! Great. He didn't want anyone's pity.

With a fierce scowl, he barked, "Don't you have a room to clean or something?"

She flinched, a wounded expression on her face. Slamming the skillet on the stove, she walked from the kitchen, chin held high.

"Aw, hell." Now he'd done it. Mark hated it when women played the guilt-trip game. Even so, the expression on her face was going to haunt him. Keith had had the same hurt and accusing look the night Mark had left home. That was the last time he'd seen his kid brother.

With years of practice, Mark pushed the memory back to the farthest corner of his mind. And he wasn't going to think about Ms. Perky either. Damn it, he'd told her he'd get the food himself, and she wouldn't leave well enough alone. Just because she had a beautiful smile and hadn't stared at him in disgust, didn't mean she wasn't like every other woman.

She'd probably summoned that trembling bottom lip just to manipulate him, the way his mom used to. Watching his mother have one affair after another, he'd learned at an early age what women were like. Why should this one be any different?

He looked at the plate of cooling biscuits and gravy and suppressed the urge to slam it against a wall. He needed a beer.

Two

Audrey held the wet washcloth against her heated face and refused to let the tears fall. She must've been delusional to think, even for a brief moment, that she'd seen attraction in Mark's eyes. Why would he be attracted to her? He'd dated some of the most beautiful women in the world. Of course he'd thought she was someone else last night.

But that didn't mean she had to hide in her bathroom like a chastised child. Why was she so upset? Who cared if a hungover, rude cowboy despised her? She was a twenty-five-year-old professional. Not the fat, lonely object of scorn she'd been the first time they'd met. Well, not *as* fat. And she'd stood up to her boss, hadn't she?

When she'd presented him with the idea for this story, Mr. Burke had laughed, his tone condescending as usual. "My mild-mannered little copy editor? You're just not ready for a story this big, Audrey. If you want to write something, how about taking over the advice column for a few months?"

Audrey had known months would turn into years, as with her current position. The only way she'd been able to convince him to give her a chance was to go for high stakes.

"Here's the deal, Mr. Burke. If I don't come back with the scoop on what happened to Mark Malone, I'll edit copy *and* do the advice column. But—" she'd flattened her palms on the desk between them, leaned in, and met his eyes with determination "—when I bring back this article, I want a staff writer position."

Mr. Burke had finally raised his hands in surrender. "All right. All right. The magazine needs a good cover story for the July rodeo issue. If you can get an exclusive interview with the *Lone Cowboy,* the position's yours."

Remembering that conversation gave her the courage to return to the kitchen. As she entered, John Walsh was just coming in the back door. Following him was a slim lady with thick white hair twisted in a stylish French roll. She wore pressed jeans and a western shirt. "You must be Audrey!" the woman exclaimed, flashing a big smile with slightly crooked teeth. "I'm Helen, John's wife."

"Nice to meet you." Audrey offered a friendly smile. "Do y'all want some iced tea?"

"Does a bull want a heifer?" John asked as he grabbed a chair and turned it around backward to sit.

"John!" Helen swatted playfully at his arm as John chuckled under his breath. Helen shook her head and gave Audrey a rueful grin. "After almost fifty years, I still can't tame him, and I sure can't shoot him."

John took Helen's hand and raised it to his lips. They exchanged an affectionate look.

It seemed to Audrey they were still very much in love. After fifty years? She dreamed of a romance like that.

Helen turned to her as Audrey poured the tea.

"We know the house is awful, but…" Helen hesitated and gave John a look charged with unspoken questions. "Mark's recuperation has been slow and, well, you can see why he needs a good housekeeper."

Slow? Now was her chance to get some straight answers. "Were his injuries severe?"

Helen frowned and dropped her gaze to the table. "Well, his right leg was crushed—"

"Crushed!" Was that why he'd been so defensive about his leg? This revelation made her more determined than ever to talk to Mark Malone. She knew this would be the story to launch her career.

"He was in the hospital for six weeks, and then physical therapy. It took another two months for him to walk again. The retirement has been…an adjustment for him."

"Well, if you ladies are through gabbing." John stood, turning his chair and pushing it in. "I've got to get back to work."

"Work?" Helen exclaimed. "I thought you were going to show Audrey around."

His eyes twinkled as he gave her a mischievous grin. "Can't spare the time. I asked Mark to do it."

Audrey heard boot steps behind her and spun to see Mark standing in the doorway, holding a beer. He scowled at John, but stepped in and bent to give Helen a quick kiss on the cheek. "How's your arthritis?"

Helen waved away his concern and stood up. "I'm fine. Got to go." She followed John out but turned on the porch. "Y'all have a good afternoon." She smiled and waved.

Audrey swallowed the lump in her throat and tried to smile back.

Mark glared at her and paced to the fridge. He opened the door, leaned in and reappeared with a fresh bottle of beer. Popping the top, he gestured toward the door. "After you."

"The Double M's over five thousand acres, and there's about twelve hundred head of brindled cattle," Mark said as he passed the corral. He took a long swallow of beer before continuing. "The extra men are here for spring roundup. Usually it's just Jim, Ruth and John."

"And you," Audrey interjected as she quickstepped to keep up with his long-legged stride.

Mark frowned and stuck the fingers of his free hand into the pocket of his jeans. "Not anymore," he muttered. He shook his head and headed for the barn, tipping the bottle to his lips again.

She trailed after him, determined to get some answers. "Why are you selling?"

His stride hitched only slightly before he took another drink and continued as if he hadn't heard her. When he reached the barn doors, he stopped and turned, his eyes sparking with annoyance. "John said you usually work for a disaster-recovery company in Dallas. What are you doing out here in hayseed country?"

Audrey was caught in his intense gaze. She opened her mouth but nothing came out. She'd stick to the truth as much as possible. "My uncle owns the company. I don't actually work there anymore." *Not since college.* "But then I saw the ad for this housekeeping position and…." Her voice trailed off. She dropped her gaze. "And I've always been a big fan."

Mark snorted and angled his head toward the barn. "We keep the hay and feed in here." He pointed his beer bottle toward the other large wooden structure. "Horses and tack in the stable. That's about it." He turned to leave.

But Audrey brushed past him and stepped into the barn. The combined smells of hay and leather reminded her of her dad. With a nostalgic smile, she wandered farther inside. She turned a corner and saw a large metal barrel with a rope tied around it, turned on its side and stuck on a metal post. There was a lever on the wall behind it, and beneath it was a thick pad extending about three feet in each direction.

"Wow. A mechanical bull!"

"It didn't have the pad at first," Mark said quietly behind her. "But when the kids came out here, I added the pad for safety."

Kids? She swiveled to stare at him. "You have children?"

His brows drew together and his mouth pinched into a tight line. "No, I meant the foster kids." Mark headed for the doors. "Coming?"

Audrey reluctantly followed. She'd read of Mark Malone's support for Big Brothers Big Sisters of America, and admired him for making a difference in the world. But she hadn't realized he'd brought the kids to his ranch. That bit of information had never been mentioned in an interview. At last! Something good for her story!

Mark escorted her to the back porch, gave her an insolent salute with his beer bottle and sauntered off toward the front of the house.

An eerie silence descended after he'd gone. Audrey shivered. She hated to deceive him, but she wasn't going to hurt anyone. Just write a little article about what had happened to a famous rodeo champion, earn herself a promotion and, hopefully, get to know a real-life hero.

If she could just put aside this niggling sense of guilt, she'd make it through this just fine.

She rubbed her arms and wandered into the den. Drawn to the wall of picture windows, she gazed wistfully out, past the neglected pool and yard to the barn and corral in the distance. A lush forest of pines, oaks and sweet gums lined the horizon.

Audrey turned to scan the gloomy room. Her heart ached at the wasted potential of the room—and its owner. A pine-paneled wall opened to a dark hallway that led to the master bedroom, and on the other side, a large stone fireplace sat alone, like the house, cold and empty. The only furniture in the room was a tattered recliner and a big-screen TV.

Well, if she were going to carry out this charade, she should start cleaning this pigsty. The cowboys'—and girl's—mud-caked jeans were piled high in the laundry room. As she put on a load to wash, a thought hit her. A real housekeeper would clean Mark's room and change the sheets. She decided to tackle that room first thing tomorrow morning.

That night at dinner, Audrey self-consciously pulled the bottom of her T-shirt down after she set a giant bowl of mashed potatoes in the middle of the table.

Thank goodness for Ruth. All this testosterone in one room left her flustered and overwhelmed. Men definitely didn't eat the way her sisters did. The meal was a loud, boisterous affair.

She learned a lot more than she ever wanted to know about ranching. Discussion of branding, ear tagging, vaccinations, calves, yearlings and castration all figured in the dinner conversation.

One of the youngest hands, Pete, had scrambled for the seat next to her. He leaned close and threw his arm across the back of her chair, caressing her shoulder. Knowing of his nomadic lifestyle, she tried to chalk it up to loneliness, and ignore him. But every time he touched her, she felt a strong urge to bathe.

"Ma'am, these chops are great!" Jim called from the other end of the table. "After working with cows all day, it's nice to not have to eat one." He stuffed a bite into his mouth.

Audrey stopped chewing momentarily as certain images came to mind. She would definitely lose some weight if there wasn't a change of subject.

"They're the best pork chops I've ever tasted," Dalt agreed with his guaranteed-to-melt-hearts smile.

She smiled back. "Thank you. There's a secret ingredient."

"Mark loves pork chops," John muttered from his seat across the table.

Mark was absent from the meal again, and she worried he wasn't eating. Why on earth did she care, anyway? But John had given her the opening she'd been waiting for.

"Mr. Malone seems to have changed a great deal since the accident," she fished.

John frowned and gave his full attention to his plate.

Audrey wouldn't let it go this time. She needed information. "Was his right leg the only injury? What's he going to do after he sells the ranch?"

John glanced up sharply, scowling.

Maybe she should act worried for his health. *Act?* "It's

just that he doesn't seem to eat. I wondered if I should take some dinner in to him."

As if they'd rehearsed it, several guys erupted into laughter at the same time.

Jim, still snickering, said, "Not unless your secret ingredient is whiskey!"

More laughter followed, but Audrey frowned with disapproval. "I don't see what's so funny about a man drinking himself into oblivion every night. You should be encouraging him to join AA or something."

That sobered them up a little, so to speak. Jim finally answered. "Beggin' your pardon, Miss Audrey, but Mark's a grown man and ain't nobody gonna tell him what to do. Besides," he continued with a grin, "I win too much money off him to wanna change things."

Ruth must've caught Audrey's confused expression. "Some of us play poker at night," she explained. "Guess with your room upstairs, you haven't heard anything."

So that explained the mess in the dining room. Poker! She didn't know what else to say, so she mumbled something about being a sound sleeper and started clearing dishes off the table.

Looking slightly guilty, the men and Ruth thanked her for the meal and shuffled out.

As she loaded the dishwasher, a horrifying thought struck her. It would make a sensational story, but if she couldn't stand to see Mark become a laughingstock to his own hired hands, how could she bring herself to write an exposé and tell the whole world about his problems?

Arms loaded with a tray containing pork chops, potatoes, broccoli and a slice of apple pie, Audrey knocked on the master bedroom door.

No answer.

She knocked again, louder.

A deep, slurred voice grumbled, "Go away!"

She rapped again and shouted through the door, "I've brought you some dinner."

Silence.

She took a deep breath for courage and shoved the door open with her shoulder.

The only light came from a metal gooseneck lamp on a small plastic table by the bed. The rest of the room was shrouded in shadow. The hand-carved pine bed and an old-fashioned armoire against one wall was the only other furniture. Empty beer bottles and dirty tumblers littered the table, and clothes were strewn on the floor. How could anyone live like this?

Mark was sitting on the side of the king-size bed, wearing only a pair of white briefs, his elbows on his knees and his forehead in his hands. His broad chest sported a light dusting of chestnut hair, and his arms and left thigh were thick with muscles. Even with the injured leg and a scruffy beard, Mark Malone was sinfully gorgeous.

Stop thinking like that! You're here for one purpose, to get the story of the Lone Cowboy!

Powerless to stop herself, she looked her fill. His right leg was shrunken, with long, jagged scars snaking around from the top of his thigh all the way to his ankle. As she stood there, she wondered where she would find the coverage to ask about his injury?

Mark glanced up and did a double take. What the hell? It was little Ms. Nosy. Couldn't she respect a man's privacy? He grabbed the sheet and threw it over his leg. Had she seen it?

"What do you want?"

She extended a huge tray of food. "Um, I brought you dinner. I thought you should eat something."

"I'm not hungry." His head ached and his leg throbbed and he didn't want her pity.

"Are you sure?" She moved closer, and the aroma of honey and garlic drifted to him. "John said you love pork chops."

Anger flared. Of course—John had put her up to this! "No, thanks." He spied a half-full beer bottle on the night-stand and reached for it.

"You don't really need that, do you? You know, drinking won't solve your problems."

"Look, lady," he sighed, his hand halted halfway to the table. "You don't know anything about my problems."

The bed dipped as she set the tray on the mattress. "My name is Audrey." She strode over to the table and grabbed up an empty beer bottle. "I'll just clear this off while I'm here." The glass bottles clanked as she filled her arms.

Mark winced. His stomach churned. His head pounded as if a bronc had kicked it. He just needed a sip to take the edge off. Before she could take it away, he leaned forward and grabbed the half-full bottle from her hand.

Damn. She had that hurt look again. Her green eyes reproached him. His gaze dropped to her full lips. She licked them and he envied her tongue. He looked back up to her eyes and leaned forward, reaching out a hand to touch her smooth cheek.

For a moment, he thought she felt the same pull he did. Her eyes closed and her mouth opened. But she jerked back and made a little sputtering sound.

Damn it! What the hell was he thinking? He looked away and started to drink.

The beer was almost to his mouth when she latched on to the bottle. "Stop! You have this beautiful ranch, and good friends, yet all you do is sit in here and drown your sorrows. There's so much more to life!"

He glared at her. "Lady, if I want a sermon, I'll go to church." He tugged on the bottle.

She didn't take the hint. "Please. This isn't the man I've admired all these years."

Who the hell does she think she is? "I'm not the *Lone Cowboy* anymore!" As if to prove his words true, his muscle cramped and pain streaked down his leg. "I can barely walk."

"Oh, please!" She let go of the beer and stalked around the room. "The point is you *can* walk. And you've got two strong arms." She grabbed clothes and bottles as she ranted. "You can do whatever you set your mind to."

"Are you through yelling?" he said, grinding out the words. He might take this from John, but he didn't have to listen to some carping housecleaner, even if she did have a cute, round behind.

She turned back to him, one hand on her hip. "No." The woman was relentless. "My brother-in-law has ALS. Lou Gehrig's disease. It attacks his muscles, and every day he loses more ability to move his arms and legs. He's in a wheelchair. He can't talk or move his hands or even swallow. He won't live to see his son grow up!" She stopped in front of him and shook her fistful of clothes at him. "Yet he gets up every morning and thanks God for one more day!"

She glanced at the empty beer bottles and dirty clothes in her arms with a look of disbelief. Her brows drew together and her eyes darted about the room as if she were amazed to find it straightened.

Mark stared at her. Her brother-in-law was dying? What

had she called it? ALS? And the poor guy had a son? What a screwed-up world. His own father had never bothered to be a part of his or Keith's lives.

He realized he still held the beer. *Ah, finally a nice, long swallow.*

She snatched his liquid relief just as he raised the bottle to his mouth again.

"What the hell?"

The interfering little tyrant stalked to the bathroom, and a second later he heard the sound of the precious fluid splashing in the sink, his hopes for a cure flowing down the drain. For a moment he sat frozen by fury until, like a volcano, he erupted, spewing every curse word he knew.

She stomped back out of the bathroom and dumped the clothes and bottles in a heap at his feet. "What a waste of a life!" A smug look of triumph illuminated her face as she sailed out of the room.

Three

A hoarse shout penetrated her sleep. Audrey rolled out of bed, grabbed her robe and scrambled down the stairs, heading toward the origin of the cry. Did her mother need another pain shot?

Audrey stopped and rubbed her eyes as she became more alert. Her mother had died eleven years ago, and she was at the Double M.

Had she dreamed the sound of someone yelling out in pain? She crept to Mark's door and listened. When she heard nothing but silence, she turned to leave.

"No!" a strangled voice called out.

She pushed open the door and raced to his side. With the light from the connecting bathroom, she could see his shadowy figure lying on the bed. He appeared to be asleep. The sheets were tangled around the lower half of his long torso, and his face and chest glistened with sweat. His hair was mussed and he twisted away with a low moan. His expression looked so tortured, he seemed a different man from the belligerent drunk of last night.

Was he reliving that night the bull crushed his leg? Or was there something else in this man's life that prompted this horrible dream?

She reached out a tentative hand to brush a strand of hair off his cheek, but checked her dangerous impulse. Her palm hovered over him for what seemed like minutes.

His arm flashed up and knocked her hand away with a coarse swearword.

Mark bolted up in a cold sweat, shaking uncontrollably. His leg throbbed. Relentless images flashed through his mind.

His mom was screaming. Mark dragged Keith to the safety of the back bedroom. His brother was only three, and didn't understand what was happening. Through the bedroom window he saw the flashing light of the police car. The medic yelled, "She's still alive," while the cops took his father away in handcuffs. Dad would never come back.

And Mark knew it was all his fault.

"Are you okay?" a soft voice asked.

Mark blinked and focused on a blurry figure a few feet away. Audrey. What was *she* doing here? Oh, God. Had he yelled in his sleep?

"Just dandy."

"Anything I can do?"

Great. Florence Nightingale to the rescue.

"No, I'm fine." He closed his eyes and winced, wishing he hadn't thrown out those pain pills the doctor had prescribed. They'd kept him blessedly numb in the hospital.

Beer. He needed a beer and an aspirin.

He threw back the sheet and started to swing his leg to the floor, but she was still there, hovering.

Why didn't she just leave? He couldn't see much, but what he saw had his blood heating up. The lush curves teased him from beneath her robe. His body hardened. At least he wasn't thinking about the nightmare anymore.

"I heard you cry out. It might help to talk about it."

Her melodic voice aroused him more. "You want to help?" He stood and put his hands on his hips, displaying his need. "Come here and kiss my troubles away."

Her gaze darted down, and the whites of her eyes got bigger like a scared filly, before her shadowy silhouette swished out of his room.

He called after her. "What'd ya expect, a hero?"

Ignoring the pain, he stood and carefully slipped on his jeans. He caught a whiff of her lingering, sultry citrus scent as he headed for the stable.

Mark flipped on the light and made his way to his stallion's stall, grabbing a brush and a bucket of oats along the way. It had been a few days since he'd checked on his horse. Lone Star nickered and tossed his head.

"Whoa, there, boy. How ya been?" He ran his hand down the stallion's flank and poured the oats into his trough. Lone Star didn't seem to mind it was three in the morning.

It might help to talk about it. What the hell did she know? Talking wouldn't help. He'd had that nightmare ever since he'd ratted on his mother. And deserting his brother had only made it worse.

Mark ran the brush across Star's back. "We had us some great times, didn't we, Star? For a while there, I could pretend I was somebody else."

He scratched the giant stallion behind the ear. "They been treating you good, boy? You lonely?" Lone Star whinnied and nudged Mark with his nose. "Yeah, me neither." Out of habit, Mark stooped to check Star's hooves. Searing pain shot through his leg. He stumbled forward, catching the horse around its neck for support. "Damn it to hell!"

Lone Star trembled, but remained steady as Mark pulled himself up and rested his forehead against the horse's neck. "I oughta sell you, boy," he whispered. "You're wasted on me."

Mark rubbed his throbbing leg as he headed for the house. Just past the barn doors he caught a whiff of… lemon. Damn it! He turned, and there she was, flattened against the barn wall like a prison escapee.

"What the hell are you doing?"

She stepped forward, clutching the front of her robe together with both hands. "I was worried about you."

"About me?" Women didn't worry about Mark Malone. They either wanted money or their fifteen minutes of fame.

"You find that so hard to believe?"

He crossed his arms. "Yeah, I do. Were you in there?" He nodded toward the barn doors.

She nodded. "I guess we both like to visit Lone Star when we need to sort things out."

"What? Lady, you've been watching too many TV talk shows!" He spun around and walked back to the dark house, putting equal weight on his throbbing leg. He'd be damned if she'd see him limp.

He slammed through the back door and headed straight for the bar. Grabbing a bottle of whiskey, he didn't even bother with a glass. He stopped in midstride, staring at his gold championship buckles on display. Bile rose in his throat, and the rage seething in his veins erupted. He raked his hand across the shelf, sending the belt buckles crashing to the floor.

Audrey awoke with a vague sense of hopelessness. Last night's incident with Mark weighed on her mind. She'd never forget the heart-wrenching pain in Mark's hoarse shout.

It was still pitch-dark when she stumbled to the kitchen to cook breakfast for what seemed like the entire U.S. Army. If she never saw a slice of raw bacon again, she'd be a happy woman. Writing the "Dear Audrey" column was beginning to seem like a dream job. It didn't look as if she'd ever get a story here, anyway. Only propositions from drunks and unsavory ranch hands.

Grumbling to herself, she set the table. Nine years ago, she'd dreamed of Mark whisking her off on his horse and living happily ever after.

How pathetic.

Over the years, the few men who had looked past her plain features and plumpness to ask her out had only wanted one thing. Even if she'd been willing to do *that* on a first date—or even a second—she would've been too embarrassed to get undressed.

She'd been fourteen when her mom died, and until recently, she'd put all her energy into taking care of her dad and two younger sisters. But Miranda had her degree now, and a hunky boyfriend, and Claire had her husband and three-year-old son.

And all Audrey had was a dead-end job.

As the sun rose in a brilliant palette of pinks and lavenders, so did Audrey's spirits. Was she going to give up now? Just because things were a little more difficult than she'd imagined? Slink back to the magazine and be taken for granted the rest of her boring life?

No way.

After breakfast Audrey dragged the vacuum cleaner to the den, intent on conquering the dust and dirt there.

Mark shuffled in with a six-pack and settled into his recliner.

She pursed her lips at the thought of him spending another day lounging in the recliner watching sports news. She glared at him and fired up the vacuum.

Snarling, he grabbed the remote and turned the volume up full blast.

She repressed the urge to seize the remote and chuck it into the pool. Or toss the vacuum at the TV screen.

Mark Malone wasn't the only one who'd had hardships in life. Surviving the loss of her mother hadn't been easy. But she certainly hadn't thrown herself a big pity party.

But she wouldn't lose her temper again. Come to think of it, now would be the perfect time to actually clean his room. She certainly wasn't going to ask him about his past this morning! She left the vacuuming unfinished, gathered her cleaning supplies and headed down the hall.

First, she raised the heavy shades that blocked out the bright morning sun from both windows. What a shame to see such a beautiful pine bed so dry and dusty. A good polish with orange oil brought the wood to a glossy shine. She remade the bed and then began dusting the armoire. On top sat a Matchbox car and an old, tattered, wallet-size picture of a little boy, about eight years old. The boy didn't look like Mark. A brother? A childhood friend? She didn't know anything about his family. And John had acted extremely suspicious when she'd asked.

She caught a movement from the corner of her eye. Jumping back, her heart banged against her chest when she glanced up and found Mark standing in the doorway, glaring.

"What the hell are you doing with that?"

With a shaky breath, she dropped the picture back on the armoire and casually moved past him to the bed, smoothing the comforter over the clean sheets.

Flexing chest muscles and a flat stomach revealed by low-riding jeans distracted Audrey from his question. Hadn't his shirt been buttoned before? It was hard to concentrate with his brown chest hair arrowing down to well-defined abs.

"Just dusting."

He raised one brow in disbelief as he lifted a bottle of beer to his lips. His Adam's apple bobbed as he took a long swallow. From her hands smoothing the comforter, his piercing gaze journeyed slowly to her chest, lingered a moment and continued to scorch over her hips and thighs.

Her facade of poise withered under his scrutiny. There was that look she thought she'd imagined last time. The flare of desire in his eyes made her feel like someone else, someone alluring and sexy.

It was awfully hot in here. Maybe she should have turned down the air conditioner. Changing sheets was hard work.

But that didn't explain the sharp ache between her thighs.

Mark's gaze shifted to the bed, then back to her. "Gonna help me get it all rumpled again?"

Audrey blinked. The romantic haze cleared from her eyes. She crossed her arms and looked pointedly out the bedroom door. "I thought you wanted to watch TV."

He smacked his lips together and wiped his mouth on his shirtsleeve. "Changed my mind."

She rolled her eyes and grimaced, biting her tongue to keep her criticism to herself.

"What? Go ahead and say it, Miss High-and-Mighty. I can see you're dying to give another lecture. You're on your own personal crippled-cowboy crusade? I suppose *you* never drink?"

"Not at ten o'clock in the morning!"

His brows drew together and his scowl blackened. He advanced on her, taking another swig from his bottle, and wiped his mouth on his sleeve again. He closed in until she was nose to chest with him, caught between him and the bed. He was so close she could smell the beer on his breath.

Refusing to be chased away, she stood her ground.

He towered over her with a narrow-eyed glare. "You know, you should've been a missionary or something. I can see you now. Marching for prohibition with all the other Miss Priss, goody-two-shoes, dried-up, old *spinsters!*"

Audrey's stomach heaved, as if someone had socked her. His words echoed in her mind—*dried-up, old spinster.* It was true. That's exactly what she was. Refusing to cry, she forgot about holding her temper. "Well, at least I don't sit around wallowing in self-pity all day!"

He leaned into her and nuzzled her neck. "You know, I kind of like you all riled up. Your eyes spit fire and your...." He stared blatantly at her chest. "I want you, darlin'."

Oh, God. Her nipples peaked of their own accord, as if straining to rub against his chest. Tiny goose bumps rose as his lips nibbled the sensitive skin of her neck. Even with the smell of beer on his breath, she wanted his arms around her and his lips on hers.

No. This drunk was not the man she'd once thought he was. She pushed against his chest. "Move, and I'll leave so you can drink yourself into a stupor in peace."

He set the bottle on the bedside table and abruptly fell forward, pushing her down with him. Arms straight, he held himself above her, his hands spread flat on the bed. Audrey lay perfectly still, trapped between his strong, flannel-clad arms. His lips parted and hovered just above hers.

"Peace is a pipe dream, baby. I'll take passion any day."

Eyes wide, she reined in the urge to grab a hunk of his hair and pull his mouth down to hers. Despite the long hair and heavy stubble, she kept seeing the handsome, smiling hero from that long-ago night at the rodeo.

"Beautiful green eyes," he mumbled. "Give me a kiss, baby." Feverishly, his lips covered hers, moving over her mouth, begging for a response.

No need to beg. Audrey ran her fingers through his hair and kissed him back with all that was in her.

He slowly lowered his body, settling onto her chest with a low groan. His tongue slid in, stroking her lips and tongue.

She shivered and couldn't hide a little moan of pleasure as his lips traveled down her cheek to nuzzle her neck. The evidence of his desire pushed against her thigh, long and hard. He pushed it against her again, and she realized his hand was sliding under her shirt.

She must be insane! A minute ago, he'd called her an old spinster. He only wanted her because he was drunk. She recovered her wits and pushed on his shoulders. "No!"

He rolled away and sat up. "What's the matter?"

Audrey bolted off the bed and flew to the other side of the room, breathing hard. She didn't know which feeling was stronger—humiliation or regret. "You don't even know me."

Grabbing his beer, he took another swig and ran a hand through his hair. "Hell, what's knowin' someone got to do with it? The women who wanted the *Lone Cowboy* didn't know me." He thumped his chest and snarled his famous moniker as if he were speaking of someone else.

Crossing her arms, she dropped her jaw in disbelief. "That doesn't mean— Oh!" Did he think because she was a fat *spinster*, she wouldn't say no?

Mark frowned and crossed his arms over his chest. "I get it. The cripple ain't good enough."

Is that what he thought? As if that would make a difference if she loved— *Don't go there, girl.* "Your injury has nothing to do with—"

"Save it, lady. I know how women are."

Audrey fumed, wishing she could scream. Why bother arguing with him? "Think what you want. *Do* what you want. But leave me alone. And I'll leave you alone, okay?" She spun on her heel, snatched up her cleaning supplies and left the room.

Mark cursed, and pitched his empty bottle on the floor. Now his room was quiet. But he could hear the vacuum whirring out in the den.

Yeah. Alone. That's what he wanted. Wasn't it? No one judging him? Or expecting more? Then why did his chest ache when she left? Why had he wanted to reach out and apologize and promise her anything if she'd stay? What the hell was wrong with him?

He straightened his spine. Nothing another beer wouldn't cure.

Audrey spent the rest of the day grumbling under her breath as she cleaned. She couldn't stop thinking about how much Mark Malone had changed. Some hero. Maybe the Double M stood for "Mad Malone." She pictured the headline, with her name underneath.

Madman Malone Massacres Meddling Magazine Journalist. She giggled, delving deep for more alliterative headlines.

Lone Cowboy Loser at Life.

Or how about: *Callous Cowboy Casts Off Comfort—* Comfort? Since when did she want to comfort him?

Audrey sighed. Since she'd seen the pain in his eyes.

Ugh! There was a full spittoon under the card table. How disgusting. What the heck was she supposed to do with that? And the carpet? She didn't want to think about it. She made a mental note to rent a carpet cleaner in Quitman, the closest town to the Double M.

Cleaning this mess was her job, but did they have to spit and smoke and drink in here? Couldn't they go out to the bunkhouse? She was tempted to discuss it with John. They wanted to sell the place, didn't they?

But maybe she'd better let it go for now. In just three days, she'd kicked her employer in his bad leg, threatened him with a knife and lectured him about his drinking.

She heaved a frustrated sigh. Besides, she'd be gone in less than a couple of weeks. She could stand anything for that long. Even rude, ex-rodeo stars.

As she snatched empty beer bottles off the floor, she glanced across the foyer to the formal living room, bare except for a wet bar with a half-full wine rack and a pile of trophies and gold belt buckles scattered across the floor. *His* championship buckles.

Now that her temper was spent, the memory of Mark's kiss caused a pang of desire. He'd actually kissed her! And called her beautiful. The beer must have blurred his vision. There was no mistaking his aroused state though. He'd admitted that knowing someone had nothing to do with wanting someone. And it must not.

Because she'd wanted him, too.

He was her employer. But the thought of suing for sexual harassment never entered her head. Then again, he hadn't fired her for pouring his beer down the sink, either.

She cringed thinking about that. And how she'd talked to him. Maybe she'd taken her new "assertive" attitude too far. If he fired her now, she'd never know the whole story. But she just couldn't stay in this house and watch him drink himself to death.

He'd obviously let the injury ruin his life. She should have mentioned professional help. She knew it was none of her business, but someone had to care enough to— Care?

What are you doing, girl, planning his rehabilitation? Where's your precious objectivity? You're a journalist, not a social worker. Get over it!

Unfortunately, that was easier said than done, and hero or not, Mark Malone was more than just a story to her. He always had been and always would be. And this whole business had the potential to ruin her new career.

Four

The next afternoon, as Audrey headed to the bunkhouse carrying neatly folded stacks of laundry, she heard hooting and laughter coming from the barn. Curley, usually at her heels, barked and rushed inside.

Audrey couldn't resist changing course to check out the commotion. Maybe in this more relaxed atmosphere they'd let something slip about Mark. She had to get to the bottom of this mystery. There must be more to this story than his injury. What could have made him change so much? Had all his endorsement opportunities dried up after the accident?

She followed the sounds back to the far corner of the barn. Dalt twisted and turned on the bucking mechanical bull, while Jim operated the lever.

After a couple of seconds, Dalt flew off and landed on his backside. When he saw Audrey watching, he jumped up, gingerly rubbing his behind. He sauntered over to her with his most charming grin. "Hey, Audrey. You wanna give it a try? I'll make sure we take it real slow." Dalt raised his brows, then actually winked—at her! Was he playing a cruel joke?

Someone taunted, "Come on, Pete, show your sack!" Pete leered at her, blew her a kiss and then climbed on the barrel.

"They were just tellin' him to, uh, to have some, uh, you know, courage," Dalt explained.

"My dad's a rodeo man, Dalt. I'm familiar with the expression."

"So, you gonna be next?" He slipped an arm around her waist, pulled her close and whispered in her ear, "I'll help you hold on, if you want."

"Oh, no. I—" A small voice buzzed through her brain, tempting her. *Why not?* it whispered. *You wanted to experience more of life, didn't you?*

"Okay." She plunked the laundry into Dalt's unsuspecting arms. "I'll need a step stool, though."

A huge grin spread over Dalt's face. "Sure, sweetheart. Whatever you want. Come on in here and we'll get you all fixed up."

Pete jumped off, and before she had time to reconsider her foolishness, she climbed on, coaxed by Dalt in his soothing southern drawl. The barrel began to rock in gentle, rhythmic motions. Audrey clenched her fists tightly around the rope. Her legs hugged the barrel so hard she could feel her thigh muscles straining.

After a few seconds, with Dalt and the other guys cheering her on, the rocking motion sped up. She concentrated on not falling off, matching her body's wits against the "bull." A powerful energy surged through her. Her heart pumped faster. This must be what Mark felt when he rode. Excited. Challenged. Unconquerable. She stuck her right arm in the air and laughed.

"Don't you have dinner to cook?" a deep voice barked.

The shouting and hooting silenced. The barrel stilled. Audrey caught her breath and jerked around to find Mark scowling at her. Her face heated as blood pounded in her temples. She knew her thighs must look even fatter, spread around the barrel. Shame and embarrassment washed over her. Why did he affect her this way?

Dalt stepped over to Mark. "I was keeping her from getting back. It's my fault."

Mark glared at her, ignoring Dalt. His breathing was ragged and his blue eyes flashed with heat.

Audrey wriggled off the barrel, conscious of his gaze following her every move. Her awkward dismount couldn't be helped, but she was determined not to be intimidated.

She strode up to him and smelled the beer on his breath. He had some nerve acting as if she was shirking her duties! "Dinner, Mr. Malone, is warming in the oven. I was just about to call everyone in to eat. But you smell like you already drank yours!" She picked up the laundry Dalt had deposited on a hay bale and stalked off toward the house.

All the men except Dalt hurried for the bunkhouse, leaving Mark to stare after her retreating figure.

And what a figure it was. He couldn't decide if he wanted to wring her neck or throw her on the ground, strip her naked and take her right there in the yard. She wouldn't give him the time of day, yet here she was, flirting with every cowhand in sight.

"You're making a big mistake, Malone."

Mark glanced at Dalt. "What the hell do you know about it?"

Dalt put his hands on his hips and shook his head. "When you want a woman, you sweet-talk her, you don't growl at her."

Mark narrowed his eyes, warning him with a look.

Dalt shrugged and walked away.

Was Audrey sleeping with Dalt? He'd only been here a few weeks, but according to the guys at the poker table, his exploits with women were legendary. Why would Audrey be immune?

Except, all week he'd watched her smile and hum while she cleaned. He'd seen her sneak leftovers to Curley, and even hug John. Stupid to feel a spark of envy toward John. She'd seemed so innocent. She'd transformed the house from a dark, gloomy wreck to a warm, glowing haven. As if all was right with the world.

He wanted that feeling. He wanted her to smile at him as she had that morning in the kitchen.

He wanted her.

"Are you sure you won't come with us?" Ruth asked Audrey one more time. It was Friday night, and all the hands were going into Quitman for dancing.

"I'm sure. I don't know how you do it. I'm exhausted. Besides, I've got a good book I want to finish." Audrey loved to dance, but it'd been a long time since she'd been to a club. And in the past, she always ended up standing around watching everyone else dance.

Ruth hesitated, leaning against the door frame with her arms folded. "A bit of advice, girl to girl." She turned and waved at Dalt to go on, then looked back at Audrey. "Stay away from—"

"You know, I was just kidding about saving myself for Mark," Audrey cut her off.

A crease appeared between Ruth's brows.

Audrey cringed. She'd just made a monumental idiot of herself.

Pushing off the door frame, Ruth finger-combed her bangs back and put on her tan cowboy hat. "I was talking about Pete. He's slime. Don't let him get you alone."

Audrey's skin chilled. "Why do you say that? Did he hurt you?"

"Hah!" Ruth laughed. "Don't worry about me. Pete won't bother me anymore. Just wanted to warn you while we had a minute alone. Be careful."

With a sick stomach, Audrey nodded and waved her off. Was Pete really dangerous? She went to the kitchen and opened a window, breathing deeply to calm her shaken nerves. A cool breeze carried the sweet smell of grass, pine and wildflowers. The fresh air soothed her.

She turned on the radio while she washed the dinner dishes. As she dried the last pot, one of her favorite songs came on. The words always made her a little misty-eyed, but it had a perfect two-step beat. She cranked up the volume and danced around the kitchen.

How her heart ached to have a man who loved her so much he'd do anything just to see her smile. The way her sister, Claire, had with her husband, Danny. Someone to dance with and hold at night. They'd have a few babies and grow old together.

She remembered the beautiful smile Mark had flashed that long-ago night at Cowtown Coliseum. He never smiled now. It was as if that smile had vanished with his rodeo career. What would it take to make him smile again?

* * *

Mark heard the music and found himself drawn to the kitchen. He thought Audrey had gone dancing with everyone else. But here she was, dancing around the kitchen, adorable in her jeans and bare feet. Her blond ponytail swayed back and forth, and her arms were held out, embracing a phantom partner.

Damn his useless leg! He couldn't even take her in his arms and whirl her around the floor. Why hadn't she gone with everyone else tonight? Even as he thought the question, he stepped closer to her.

"Oomph!" He grimaced as she bumped into him. Her eyes were closed and she obviously hadn't seen him. What was his excuse?

She grabbed his arms and steadied herself. "Oh, I'm sorry! I wasn't watching where I—"

He suppressed a shiver as she ran her hands down his arms. His sleeveless sweatshirt offered no protection against the soft caress of her hands on his flesh.

She dragged in a ragged breath, bolted to the sink and stood gazing out the window.

Had he seen tears in her eyes? Without thinking, he followed her. *Wait a minute, Malone. She's already rejected you once.*

Still, he was tired of her disdain and their angry truce.

He lowered his face to her hair and inhaled the scent of lemons. He longed to place his lips on the back of her neck. No. He fisted his hands. He wouldn't touch her. "What's wrong?" he whispered in her ear.

Now she'd say, "Nothing," as all women did. Then she'd slyly mention what she really wanted. Probably money.

She turned around, eyes on the floor as she wiped at her cheeks. "It was just that song." Her lips trembled as she tried to smile. "It's stupid to cry over a song, isn't it?" With a choked laugh, she started sobbing.

No, don't...don't cry. Don't lean into me. Don't you know I can't help you?

With a frustrated growl, he wrapped his arms around her and let her weep into his shirt. Whispering soothing words, he brushed his hand down the crown of her head and across her shoulders. She was so soft and rounded. Her breasts pressed against his chest, and he wanted to feel them in his palms. But she needed comfort now, not lust. He concentrated on keeping his hands on her back and continued murmuring soothing noises.

This wasn't so bad. This was something he could do, even with a bum leg. She trusted him. Needed him.

When her sobs had run their course, she raised her head and stared at him, her lashes still wet with tears. The contempt usually sparking in her eyes was gone. Only pain and longing softened them now. He leaned down and gently kissed them dry. Hesitant, he pulled back to check her reaction.

Her eyes were wide and her lips were parted in a questioning look.

A fierce desire swept through him, stronger than the need for the fiery liquid he poured down his throat. He lowered his mouth to hers, kissing her with all the hunger he'd pent up since she'd first smiled at him. She tasted like strawberries and innocence, and he wanted more. With a low moan, he drew her lips even deeper into his mouth.

She shivered and opened her mouth, and he pushed his tongue in, swirling it around hers and across the inside of her lips. Her arms came around his neck, and she pressed her body close against him. Damn it all to hell! The feel of her soft curves against him was more than he could handle. He lost control.

He swung her around and pushed her against the island, squeezing her soft, generous bottom and grinding his hips against hers.

Oh God, he'd missed a woman's body! Every night this week, through a drunken haze, he'd dreamed of her in his arms like this. Still kissing her fiercely, he brought his hand up to one beautiful breast.

She jerked her lips from his, flattened her palms against his chest and shoved him away.

He lost his balance and had to take a step back with his good leg, throwing his arm behind him to grab the edge of the sink. Before he could reach for her, she raced from the kitchen and up the stairs.

What the hell had he been thinking? *Get it into your thick head, Malone. You're not the Lone Cowboy anymore.* All the *buckle bunnies* have moved on to the next big rodeo star. No woman was gonna be interested in plain old Mark Malone. A white-trash guy with a mutilated leg, a guy who had betrayed his own family.

Guilt had a way of sucking the passion right out of a person. Audrey paced in her room and berated herself. She was on the same evolutionary scale as pond scum for lying to Mark Malone.

But when Mark had kissed her, she'd responded with an intensity she'd never experienced before. His lips had sparked a trail of fire that had inflamed her entire body. His kisses had awakened her, as if she was finally alive instead of wandering numbly through a sham of a life. His strong arms surrounding her, he'd tenderly kissed her tears away. The concern in his eyes had made her knees weak.

Tonight she'd caught a glimpse of a different man. There had been passion, yes. But there'd also been compassion.

Here was the man who had braved five rowdy rednecks to rescue her. She'd not been wrong to hope he was still that man.

Audrey finally went through the motions of preparing for bed, squeezing toothpaste on her brush. *Let's get real here.* It was a pity kiss. Poor little fat girl staying at home because no one asks her to dance. Ooh, it hurt to be so honest. And she hated that he'd seen her so vulnerable.

But hadn't she seen him writhing in the throes of a nightmare, tormented and in deep pain? She'd suspected that underneath the drinking and belligerence, he hid a secret. Something besides the crushed leg had made him give up on life.

That *something* was what she needed to find out. And the only way she would was by getting him to talk. The hands probably didn't know, and though John and Helen might, they were too loyal to share Mark's private demons with her.

But could she betray him now?

She wanted this promotion to staff writer. She was determined to be more assertive, to go after her dreams. The emptiness, the loneliness, of the past few years loomed in her future.

She got into bed. Sleeping was impossible. She was restless. Edgy. Thoughts whirled through her mind. Her emotions were in turmoil. She'd been here almost a week. What was she going to do? Give up on her ambitions just because a handsome cowboy kissed her in a moment of sympathy?

She heard raucous laughter coming from downstairs. Guess the guys were back from town.

Men! It still infuriated her that they smoked and spit and threw their trash all over the place. If they had to play poker why couldn't they—

Poker! Of course. This way, it would be less of a betrayal and more like a challenge. Mark would have a choice. A simple, winner-take-all game. All she had to do was wait for a winning hand and the right moment, and force him to bet an exclusive interview. It would be a relief to be honest about why she was really there.

She showered and dressed, purposely wearing the one blouse she owned with a low neckline.

Audrey figured she'd need all those acting skills she hadn't used since her tenth-grade drama class to pull this scheme off. When the men turned to stare at her as she walked into the dining room, she almost lost her nerve. She tried to stop her voice from shaking when she said, "I couldn't sleep. Mind if I watch?"

A chorus of male voices answered, "Sure!" and, "Yeah!" at the same time. Dalt jumped up to get her a chair from the kitchen.

Mark's usual scowl grew even darker. Gone was the compassionate man from a few hours ago.

"Oh, thank you." She sat across from Mark, folded her arms on the table and leaned forward. Her father had taught her that an important tool in winning a poker game was distraction. Might as well use the only asset she had. She was out to win.

She felt the men's gazes drop to her chest. "I used to play cards with my family when we were younger, and it was really fun."

With a small sigh of relief, she could tell her ploy was working with predictable ease. Both Dalt and Jim tried to coax her into playing "just a couple of hands." Pete hadn't raised his eyes from her chest yet. The lecher.

Thank goodness Ruth wasn't playing tonight. Audrey

knew another woman would have seen straight through her act.

Mark didn't say a word. He narrowed his eyes and raised a beer bottle to his mouth for a long swallow.

"Well, you'd have to tell me what beats what and all that stuff. Sure you don't mind?" *Don't overdo it, girl!*

Several noes were drowned out by a bellowing "Hell, yes!" Mark slowly lowered his scorching gaze to her chest.

A tense silence hung over the table before Dalt challenged his boss. "Come on, Malone, let her play. What's the harm?"

Glowering at Dalt, Mark finished his beer and twisted the top off another. Finally, he gave a disgusted snort. "I can't believe y'all are gonna fall for this Little-Miss-Innocent act." He shifted his eyes to her and said, "Fine. Join us if you must."

Audrey pretended to listen intently as Jim explained about two pair and three of a kind. She even went so far as to get a pad from the kitchen and take notes.

Dalt shuffled the deck, slid it over to Mark to cut and then dealt everyone five cards. Audrey picked hers up and kept her face blank as she fanned them out. Two jacks, an ace and two sevens!

Mark opened with five dollars, and everyone stayed except Jim, who folded. Mark then raised five dollars and everyone stayed.

Audrey let go of the ace, hoping for a full house. When she got back a seven, she purposely let her excitement show. Pulling a twenty-dollar bill from her pocket, she raised the stakes and everyone folded.

She played it low-key for a while, and kept them guessing by folding with a fairly good hand or blundering a bluff.

Several hours later, Audrey had a considerable stack of

cash sitting in front of her. It was difficult to conceal a triumphant gleam behind a look of innocent amazement at her beginner's luck. Of course, it helped that all her opponents had been guzzling beer all night.

"Well, that does it for me." Dalt stood and stretched, throwing in his cards.

One by one, the other men left the table. Jim had said he had to be up early and left around one-thirty. Pete had drifted off soon after that when he ran out of money.

Audrey glanced at the clock. It was after three in the morning and she and Mark were the only players left.

Mark dealt the next hand, and Audrey picked up three queens and two fives. This was the hand she'd been waiting for. As the bidding started, she continually raised the stakes until she knew Mark had bet all the cash he had. Perfect. The time was right.

"I'll see your ten dollars and raise you, let's see, um, oh, what the heck, I'm feeling wild. I'll just throw in this whole big stack of money." She looked at Mark and gave him her best smile.

Mark leaned forward and glared at her. "I don't have that much money left."

No IOUs were allowed. Probably because, Audrey guessed, it would give Mark an unfair advantage.

She took a sip of her iced tea, to wet her suddenly dry throat, and said a little prayer. With a casual wave of her hand, she said, "Well, I guess if you don't want to fold, you could bet something besides money."

Audrey saw Mark's jaw muscle working as he gritted his teeth. His scowl grew menacing. "What do you want?"

She stopped smiling and looked directly into those tormented blue eyes. "I want…" Her gaze slid away, faltering under the guilt.

Say it, Audrey! An exclusive interview. Your life story.

She couldn't. She couldn't force the words out. She couldn't bear to see the look of betrayal in his eyes. He suspected something. But that was just it. He acted like he always expected the worst of people, and she didn't want to be another person who let him down.

"I want…" she forced her gaze back to his "…you to…stop drinking." Of course! That's what she really wanted. For him to be the man he once was. That's the story she'd write.

His eyes widened. "What?"

She braced herself for the storm. "And shave that god-awful beard!"

Mark slammed his cards on the table and hollered, "What the hell kind of bet is that?"

"Well, if you don't think you can do it…."

"I can quit drinkin' any time I want!"

Remembering that day in the barn with the mechanical bull, Audrey took a deep breath, lowered her chin and looked at him with an evil grin. "Come on, Mark. Show your sack!"

She knew what part of the male anatomy this term referred to, and it took all her willpower not to run to her room and lock the door. For one terrifying moment, she thought he might reach across the table and grab her throat with his bare hands. His eyes narrowed to slits and his upper lip curled in a snarl.

He took a deep breath as he slowly composed his expression. Keeping eye contact with her, he leaned back in his chair and one side of his mouth rose in a dangerous imitation of a smile.

That frightened her more than the thought of being found out.

He grabbed his beer and took a long, deliberate swallow before he said quietly, "Let's see..." He studied the money in the middle of the table. "I calculate you got about seventy-five dollars there. That may be worth taking a razor to my throat, but not giving up my beer. If you want to play for high stakes, you'll have to offer me something more."

"W-what do you mean?"

Mark clasped his hands behind his head. He looked smug, as if he sensed her uncertainty. "I'll see your bet by shaving my beard. And I raise you by pouring out the booze. Now you can see my raise with something I want, or fold."

"Uh, maybe we shouldn't...."

"Oh no," he cut in. "This game just got real interesting." He narrowed his eyes and jerked his chin. "You started it, you can finish it."

She was trapped. Surely he didn't want.... "You, um, want me to go on a diet?"

His eyes smoldered as he slowly shook his head. "I think you know what I want, Audrey. I want you in my bed. Tonight. Now, do you fold? Or play?"

The room began to spin and she couldn't breathe. She closed her eyes to escape those piercing blue ones. She'd come this far. She couldn't quit now. She had her pride, too.

She opened her eyes and looked at her cards. He couldn't possibly beat her full house, could he? She straightened her spine, stuck her chin out and looked at him. "Okay." Her voice wobbled and she cleared her throat. "I call. If I lose, I'll sleep with you."

Five

Damn, the woman had spunk! Mark should've felt triumphant. He knew his straight flush was practically unbeatable. But she was acting like some sacrificial virgin standing at the edge of a volcano. *Is this the only way you can get a woman, Malone? Do you really want her this way?* His stomach burned.

What did she really want? Was this because of the kiss in the kitchen? Would she really risk her precious virtue to get him to stop drinking?

He'd wanted her since she'd smiled at him that first morning, her beautiful emerald eyes shining with excitement. But not like this. He had no doubt she'd pay up if she lost. That stubborn tilt to her chin would see her through. But there were tight lines around her mouth, and her eyes were filled with apprehension.

Maybe if he became the *Lone Cowboy* again, she'd

come to him willingly. He wanted her excited, her eyes flaming with passion. His chances of that happening to-night were less than the chances of him ever getting another straight flush.

Who was this force of nature who'd found a way to make him care? He realized he didn't know anything about her. Not even her last name.

He leaned forward. "What've ya got?"

Audrey's face wavered between smug and worried as she spread her cards. "Full house, queens high."

Aw, hell. Before he had time to change his mind, he tossed his cards across the table, scattering them. He scowled at Audrey and threatened, "Don't expect to win the next one, darlin'."

A week later, Mark was cursing that poker game. Muttering a string of obscenities, he glided the razor up his neck. He'd planned on growing the beard once he sold the ranch. His face was too recognizable without it, and he'd wanted no reminders of his past. Damn it! He threw the razor into the sink and bent over, leaning on one hand. Why had he thrown that game? He'd had her right where he'd wanted her. Jeez, he wanted a beer. No, he wanted *her*. But a drink would have to do.

Mark strode to the living room, hoping Audrey would see him, daring her to say something. But no one stopped him. He stepped behind the bar, grabbed a bottle of whiskey, and unscrewed the lid. Closing his eyes, he raised it to his lips. A pair of green eyes filled with contempt and loathing swam before his closed lids. *Gonna add welshing on bets to your list of sins, Malone?*

To hell with this! He slammed the bottle on the bar and

stalked back to his room. Why did he care what she thought of him?

He'd avoided her intense eyes and voluptuous body all week. He barely managed a civil conversation with John, and he refused to alienate Audrey by snarling at her. Thinking of her passion-sated body lying in his rumpled bed was the only thing that made it worth this trouble.

The past week, he'd drunk enough iced tea to piss out a west Texas grass fire. He'd also done a lot of thinking. Looking back on his behavior over the last few weeks was worse than climbing in the chute with a rank bull. Shame filled his throat with bile at the thought of facing everyone. But John was right. He needed to cowboy up and get on with it.

He'd survived worse than a lost career, hadn't he?

He owed John an apology. He owed John and Helen a lot more than that, but he could never repay them. Just two more on the list of people he'd let down. Mark grabbed the razor from the sink and finished shaving as best he could. He'd go see John now. Before he left his room, he rummaged around in his closet and pulled out his Stetson.

The *Lone Cowboy* was back.

When Helen opened the door of her small house, Mark could smell bacon frying. He stood a moment before he remembered and took off his hat.

"Mark! Come on in." Though she recovered quickly, Mark had noticed her eyes widen in shock when she first saw him. "What are you doing here so early? Is everything okay?" Helen motioned him in, linking her arm through his as they walked toward the kitchen. He glimpsed a faint smile of approval.

"Fine. Is John busy?"

Helen squeezed his arm and beamed at him. "He's in the kitchen. Come on back and I'll get you some coffee."

John sat at the small kitchen table reading the paper, sipping from a steaming cup. Glancing up, he did a quick double take, but erased his shocked expression immediately. Before Mark asked, John stood and said, "Let's go into the study."

"I'll have breakfast ready when y'all are done," Helen said. "And I'll cut your hair for you after you eat, if you want." She handed Mark his coffee and winked.

John entered his study and motioned for Mark to sit. He folded his arms across his chest and sat on a corner of his big, scarred oak desk, but didn't speak.

Mark stood for a moment, sipping his coffee, remembering John's study in the Walsh's old house back in Fort Worth. As a kid, Mark had always loved going in there with John. This one looked exactly the same.

He looked around the room, examining the books that filled the shelves on two walls. There were the same red leather chairs with the brass buttons around the edges, the same old-fashioned globe in the brass stand in the corner and the same feeling of refuge and peace.

It smelled the same, too. Like old leather and furniture polish and a hint of fine cigar.

On the wall behind the desk was a large framed picture of Mark taken astride a bucking bull. The bull's back legs kicked up six feet in the air, with a cloud of dust behind it. Mark's left arm was raised behind him, and his right hand, in a thick leather glove, gripped the rope tied around the bull's body. He'd worn the same black cowboy hat he carried now, and had his chin tucked into his chest in a look of steely determination.

He hadn't seen that picture in a long time. Looking at it made his chest hurt. His rodeo days were over. Could he recapture the grit of that man on the bull? He looked away and sat down.

John broke the silence. "What's going on?"

Mark looked at him and shifted in his chair. "First of all, I owe you an apology for being such an ass these last couple of weeks." He lowered his gaze to his hat, shifting the brim round and round in front of him. "I can't believe you put up with my crap for this long."

John's eyes were suspiciously moist when Mark finally looked up. John cleared his throat. "I don't quit on the people I love. Apology accepted."

John had never told Mark he loved him. That was probably the closest he'd ever come to it. But it was enough. Mark had never told John he loved him, either. Come to think of it, he'd never said those words to anyone. Probably never would. "I've decided I want to keep the Double M. Will you stay on?"

John walked over to look out the window as the faint light of dawn crawled over the land. "No more booze? You gonna work the ranch?"

Fair questions, all things considered. But Mark hated being doubted. "You have my word."

John turned and offered his right hand. "Then I'll stay. Good to have you back."

After he left John and Helen's, Mark parked his truck in the garage and went straight to the stables. He hadn't ridden Lone Star since the accident. Hadn't even considered whether he could. What if he fell flat on his face? How the hell had he gotten in this predicament?

Oh, yeah. Audrey.

He saddled up Lone Star and led him out of the stable. The stallion was frisky after months of being corralled. Mounting was tricky, but after a few false starts, Mark felt steady enough in the saddle to walk around the paddock.

His hands trembled and his stomach clenched. God, his leg was so damn weak. And it hurt like hell. But if he wanted Audrey in his bed, he'd have to be the rodeo champion she thought he was. When he imagined making love with her, his need for a beer evaporated like the water in a stock tank in July.

He gripped the reins tighter and kicked Star to a trot. Soon he was racing across the pastures trying to outrun the demons that had chased him for two decades. He'd missed the wind in his face and the smell of horse. And there was a hint of rain in the air. Was it April now? The bluebonnets would be in bloom. He caught sight of a separated calf and roped him on the third try. Maybe he could do this.

Is this what the love of a good woman did to a man?

He checked that thought. Love? Hell, Audrey didn't love him. She just wanted the *Lone Cowboy*. His new housekeeper was no saint. She'd gotten what she wanted. He was clean-shaven and sober. Now that he was, he'd persuade her to come to his bed freely—not because of a bet. She'd responded to his kisses, melting and burning all at once. That wasn't something you could fake.

The Lone Cowboy would get back in the saddle in more ways than one. He wanted to crush her in his arms, bury himself inside her and take her again and again, until they were both spent. Then wake beside her in the morning and have her again. Just thinking about that was enough to start his blood racing south.

What was she doing now? He had to see her. He tugged the reins around and galloped Lone Star home.

* * *

It was time to leave. Audrey's bags were packed and sitting in the foyer. If she left now, she could arrive in Fort Worth in time to have lunch with her dad at the Cattleman's Club. Then Sunday could be spent writing up her piece for the magazine.

She was due back at work Monday with story in hand. And she had one. Not an in-depth interview, but a story nonetheless. The story of a man who struggled to walk again after months of surgeries and physical therapy.

As far as she could tell, Mark had honored their bet. Mark had avoided her all week, denying her the chance to explain about her promotion and the need for a story. But she wasn't sure she would have had the nerve to confess, anyway.

The hands had just headed for the fields when Helen walked in. "Good morning, dear."

"Good morning." Audrey reached into the cabinet for two mugs and motioned for Helen to sit. "I'm glad you're here. I wanted to say goodbye." She poured them both some coffee, feeling more lonely than when she'd arrived.

Helen looked up from her coffee, frowning. "Must you leave today?"

Audrey stared down into hers. "I should get back. I have another…" She hated lying to Helen. But neither could she admit the truth.

"Mark stopped by this morning," Helen saved her from having to choose. "I haven't seen him out of bed at that time of day in weeks. Not to mention sober." Helen rushed on, excitement lighting her eyes. "He told John he's keeping the ranch!"

Mark wasn't selling? A spark of hope lit in her heart. He was going to be okay. This ranch was a part of him. He belonged here.

"Are you sure you couldn't—"

"No." Audrey cut her off and stood to pace across the kitchen, hating to see the joyful expression on Helen's face disappear. "This was always meant to be a temporary job."

Helen stirred her coffee, gazing into her mug. "You know, when you first came here, I had a feeling you were just what this place needed. You don't know how worried John and I have been. Mark changed so much after the accident. It was like he'd given up on life."

Audrey turned and leaned on the counter. "Yes, but why? Rodeo's a dangerous sport. Dozens of cowboys get injured, some permanently. Yet they remain positive. A few even stay involved in the circuit."

Why had Mark started drinking? Was it only the loss of his career? Or was there, as she suspected, something more, something to do with his nightmare and that picture on his armoire.

Helen frowned. "Mark is quiet, reserved. I always thought his nickname had more to do with his preference for being alone than a play on his name. He never let anyone close. Never let anyone help." She looked at Audrey with admiration in her eyes. "I don't know what's going on between the two of you, but I know this—he's back among the living. And I think it has something to do with you."

Audrey dropped her gaze to the counter. Shame dug in and clutched at her heart. She'd lied to Helen. And now the dear lady thought she was some sort of saint. But she was a fraud.

"Oh, dear, has Mark ruined his chance with you?"

Audrey felt the tears on her cheeks and swiped them away. How on earth could she tell this sweet woman the truth? She shook her head. "No, no, it's nothing like that." Grabbing the empty mugs from the table, she took them to the sink and turned on the water. "Helen, how long have you known Mark?"

"Since he was just a kid. His family lived next door to us. Why?"

"There's something else you're not telling me, isn't there? I mean, I know he can't ride anymore, and that's got to be frustrating, but…" Audrey gazed out the window, thinking aloud. "He had product endorsements, the charities and this place. He was probably close to retiring, anyway. And it's not like he's in a wheelchair. He doesn't even use a cane."

Audrey turned and Helen lowered her eyes, tracing the tablecloth pattern with her finger.

"You know, don't you?" Audrey said quietly.

When Helen looked up, there were tears in her eyes. "You'll have to ask Mark."

Audrey's shoulders drooped, weighted with dread. "It was something awful, wasn't it?"

"Only Mark can tell you, dear."

"Like he'd tell me," she muttered. She whirled back around to the sink, washing the mugs to distract her from ominous thoughts. Looking up, she glanced out the window and saw one of the ranch hands riding up. She did a swift double take when she got a good look at the man.

It was Mark on Lone Star!

"H-he's riding!" Audrey whispered, clutching the counter for support before her knees gave out.

Helen stood and came to put her arm around Audrey's shoulders, flashing a grin. "Miracles do happen. Maybe you shouldn't give up so easily, dear."

Six

Audrey watched Mark slow his stallion to a walk. God, she loved watching the man ride a horse. The way his hips moved in the saddle and his thigh muscles bunched to control his mount. He halted at the back porch and dismounted slowly, easing his right leg over and down with a grimace, and then tied the reins at the railing.

When he stepped into the house, her stomach did a little flip. She couldn't speak.

Mark scowled. "Hell, I nearly killed myself shaving this morning." He pointed at himself. "Isn't this what you wanted?"

He looked so different with his clean-shaven jaw and short haircut. He was still a little pale, but determined, strong and sexy as hell in that black Stetson and those tight Wranglers.

Luckily, Helen filled in the silence. "Well, there's a

proper greeting. Where'd you learn your manners, boy, in a barn?"

Mark yanked his hat off and turned to Helen. "Sorry. Guess I need some practice in that department." His serious gaze traveled back to Audrey. He took a deep breath and cleared his throat. "I was just on my way to the north pasture. Thought I'd get somethin' to drink. Uh, water, I mean."

But he didn't move.

Helen pushed away from the table and stood. "I just remembered I've got a pie to bake." She headed for the door, but turned back. "Mark, see if you can convince Audrey to stay a while. She's planning on leaving today."

"Helen!" Audrey glared at Helen. If looks could kill, the foreman's wife would be in ICU right about now.

"Leaving?" Mark scowled again.

Helen grinned and winked at Audrey behind Mark's back. "Y'all have a good morning. I'll talk to you later."

How could Helen do that to her? What did Audrey do now? What a moron she was, just standing there, staring at him. She wanted to confess, to tell him her real reason for being there, but she couldn't.

In two strides he was at her side, his eyes locked on hers. "You're not going to leave before the party tonight, are you?"

Hmm. That cologne. It was the same musky scent he'd worn the night he'd rescued her. She couldn't catch her breath. "The party's tonight?"

He leaned closer. "The temporary hands are leavin'."

"Oh, yeah. That's right." *And so am I.*

"We need to talk."

Talk? Did he know why she was really here? He couldn't, or he'd have thrown her out.

"About what?"

He brought his hand up and caressed her cheek with his knuckles. "Us," he whispered.

She closed her eyes and swallowed. *Us?* She imagined for a moment all the possibilities in that word. Mark and Audrey. A couple. Dating. Meeting each other's families. The fantasy was absurd, but deep inside exhilaration, anticipation thrummed through her body. His hand traveled down her throat. "Jim's bringing barbecue from town."

Audrey raised her face. "That's…good," she whispered. Her skin tingled where he touched. Maybe just for tonight…

He stepped away. "So, I'll see you tonight."

Her eyes snapped open, and she almost pitched forward.

He'd put his hat on and turned to leave. Then he stopped and turned back. Grabbing her around the waist, he pulled her against his length and brought his mouth over hers for a deep kiss.

Before she could catch her breath, he let her go and left the kitchen.

He forgot his water, Audrey thought in a daze. But Mark had already mounted his stallion and ridden away.

Helen came back that afternoon and, to Audrey's surprise, had two pies with her. She smiled and raised her brows. "So you decided to stay?"

"Just for the party. I'll leave in the morning."

Helen accepted her answer with a nod. "I knew he could convince you to stay," she mumbled under her breath.

Let Helen believe what she would, but Audrey had to discover what Mark wanted to talk about. Maybe she could find the courage to tell him she worked for a magazine, and ask for an interview. She refused to run off like a coward and not finish what she'd started.

Audrey and Helen made gallons of iced tea, and set up tables in the backyard. Someone set a CD player and speakers on the porch, Jim brought the barbecue and John set a keg of beer out by the pool.

The party was in full swing when Ruth approached Audrey and handed her a beer. Audrey took a big sip just as Ruth said, "Hey, girl. I heard you and Mark were the only ones left at that poker game the other night. What happened?"

Ruth slapped her on the back a couple of times as Audrey choked. To Audrey's horror, Ruth broke into a deep laugh and looked over to where Mark stood. "I don't blame you for wantin' to check out his, uh, 'breeding methods.' Just remember my warning."

Audrey considered the odds of God granting her a favor and making a hole appear to swallow her up. She had to distract the cowgirl—quick. Looking over Ruth's shoulder, she spied another interesting source of bunkhouse gossip. "So, what's the deal with you and Dalt? Anything serious?"

Ruth took a quick look behind her. "With Dalt? Mr. Haven't-met-a-woman-I-couldn't-seduce? He's definitely not into serious. But horses ain't the only thing he knows how to handle." Ruth turned knowing eyes on Audrey.

Dalt sauntered over and pulled Ruth into a two-step. Audrey remembered all the school dances she'd stood around waiting and waiting for some boy to ask her out on the floor. Her throat tightened.

Her emotions were out of control. Guilt assaulted her conscience. She'd lied to all these nice people. And what did Mark want to talk about? It couldn't be anything good.

From the corner of her eye, she saw him. Mark held a plastic cup of iced tea, and was talking to Bill Kingston, the owner of the feed store in Quitman. He had one thumb hooked in the pocket of his jeans and his hat pushed back on his head. His blue western shirt matched his eyes, and he was so handsome it hurt. As if he sensed her stare, he turned to look at her.

Somehow, things were turned around. Tonight, Mark was the upstanding citizen and she was the self-pitying jerk.

She couldn't stay in this crowd one more second. She looked away and slowly made her way past the barn and bunkhouse.

It was a clear night with a waning moon and a blanket of twinkling stars overhead. You didn't see stars like these in the city, with all the lights and pollution. She became aware of crickets chirping and frogs croaking, and the sound of the breeze rustling through the trees. The serenity of the pine trees beckoned her like arms waiting to embrace her troubled soul. Audrey kept walking, losing herself in the beauty of the country.

She came to a stop at a creek bank. The gurgling of water over stones and the sweet smell of new grass calmed her. Nature had a way of putting things in perspective. She sat and wound her arms around her upraised knees.

She knew what was really bothering her—she didn't want to leave. Maybe if she'd finished that beer, she'd have had the guts to tell Mark the truth. What if she told him now and he threw her out in front of everyone at the party?

Leaves and twigs rustled and a shadow moved from behind a tree to her right as a figure approached. Fear immobilized her.

"You all alone out here, Audrey?" Pete came closer, stopping only a couple of feet away.

Too late she realized she'd been an idiot to come out here alone. Hadn't Ruth warned her? "Uh, well, I was just about to head back. Ruth is waiting for me to, uh…" She put her hand down and started to stand.

Before she could get fully to her feet, he lurched closer and grabbed her shoulders. "Why'd you come out here? You wanted me to follow, didn't you?" She struggled to escape his hands, but he slid one arm around her back and pulled her against him with a wiry strength. His foul breath hit her cheek as he dipped his head and planted a sloppy kiss on half her mouth.

"Pete, no." She shoved with all her strength, but he didn't budge. Her heartbeat raced as he growled and swooped down again. This time she barely avoided his mouth.

"You aren't serious about saving yourself for that crippled old has-been, are ya?" He spat out the words as he fought to kiss her. "He's been holed up here for so long he'd screw the first thing that held still long enough."

A wave of nausea hit her. Struggling was getting her nowhere. Time for extreme measures. Position the knee, aim for the groin….

"What are you doin' out here? Everything all right?"

Oh, that deep, husky voice. Audrey had never been so glad to hear it.

Pete dropped his hands and backed away. "Just talking, man. Everything's cool."

She needed a moment to compose herself. She stayed where she was, gazing at the creek.

Pete turned his head and spit into the grass. "See ya later, Audrey." He strolled back toward the party.

She heard Mark move closer and straightened her dress. There was a minute of tense silence. Had he seen her fighting Pete off? Did he think she'd been a willing participant in that?

"Was he botherin' you?" Mark's voice shook. He stalked past her, heading after Pete. "I'm gonna knock that punk from here to next Sunday."

She grabbed the back of his shirt. "No!" Pete would be leaving tomorrow. No sense in Mark making a scene at the party.

Mark swiveled to face her. "You sure you're okay?"

"I'm fine. Just tired. Had a busy day." She hoped her voice sounded normal. She tried to step away, put some distance between them. Big mistake. She didn't watch where she was going. She tripped over her own feet and started to pitch backward.

"Whoa, there." He caught her in his arms and didn't let go.

His big hands held her shoulders just as Pete's had, but she wasn't afraid. Beneath her dress, her skin burned. She ached. Audrey looked into his eyes. They seemed black in the moonlight, and still sparked with temper. Her gaze traveled down to his close-shaven jaw, and over to his chiseled, masculine lips. They parted, and she became aware of his ragged breathing. The breeze shifted, and she smelled the musky, clean scent of his cologne. Barely aware of her actions, she rose on tiptoe and buried her nose in his neck, inhaling until she was dizzy.

Mark moaned under his breath, turning his face to nuzzle against her cheek. He stepped closer, spread his legs and wrapped his arms around her waist, hugging her tight. He brought his palms up to cradle her face and crushed his mouth to hers for a long, hard kiss.

His lips were warm, strong and soft at the same time. Her arms stole around his neck and she angled her head to deepen the kiss. This was so right. No hidden motives or games, only a soul-deep longing for him.

Too soon, he pulled away and looked her in the eyes. "I called your company today and let them know you're stayin' here."

"What?" Did workers' comp cover panic attacks?

He shrugged. "The place needs a housekeeper. And you and I have some unfinished business."

What unfinished business? He must know! As upset as she was, she couldn't begin to sort through all the implications of his announcement. Would Mr. Burke think she had quit? And who did Mark think he was, calling Uncle Bill without asking her? He had no right.

But hadn't she been depressed at the thought of leaving and never seeing him again? Did she want to stay?

Stay? Her heart dropped to her stomach at the thought. Suddenly a lifetime of waking before dawn, cooking and cleaning for a dozen hungry ranch hands didn't sound that bad if it meant being with Mark Malone every day.

Was she in love with Mark?

Hah! It would be ridiculous if it weren't so…true. Love? No, no, no. This was just a response to his attentions. He'd kissed her and made her feel desirable. No one had ever done that before. She was just flattered and grateful.

He was a grouchy, overbearing—handsome, tender and sexy…. Enough! So he was all that. So what? Was she seriously considering giving up a career as a journalist— okay, copy editor—in Dallas just to scrub pots and pans in the middle of nowhere? Besides, she was living a lie. She couldn't do that.

"I can't do that," she said, pushing away from him.

He let her go. "Your uncle says you can. I doubled your salary, and he accepted a finder's fee."

She looked back up, her mind spinning. "But I, I have to be in Dallas on Monday for, uh, another job."

"He said to tell you not to worry, he'd take care of your other assignment."

What the heck did that mean? Had Uncle Bill talked to Mr. Burke? Was their deal off? Was she fired? Why did Mark want her to stay? Was he impressed with her spectacular housekeeping skills? She thought not.

It didn't matter why. She just couldn't do it. Even if she were willing to alter her life, she couldn't stay here without telling him the truth. The thought of telling him why she was really here made her short of breath. He'd hate her for deceiving him.

"No." She backed away. "There must be some mistake. I can't stay here. I just can't!" She half stumbled, half ran toward the house.

Mark wanted to roar his frustration to the sliver of moon just breaking the tree line. Or better yet, jump in the creek and cool his heated flesh.

He'd watched Audrey at the party, standing on the fringes of the yard, talking to Ruth. The sight of her in that green cotton dress, with her soft hair curling around her face and those full, red lips had had him painfully aroused all night.

He felt like he was back in eighth grade, when a glimpse of one of the cheerleaders in her skimpy little skirt forced him to step into the bathroom and make a few adjustments.

When he'd caught Audrey in his arms, fire had rushed through his veins. When she'd started snuggling into his neck, he'd gone beyond the call of duty not taking her right there in the grass.

And Audrey had wanted him, too, the way she'd leaned in and opened her mouth, asking for more. What kind of game was she playing now? And what the hell had she been doing out here with Pete? Had she arranged to meet him out here and then changed her mind? The kid was barely shaving.

Of course, that had never stopped Mark's mom. She'd paraded so many men through their house, it's a wonder he'd ever gotten any sleep.

A vivid memory flashed through him. It was winter and he was small, around five. He remembered her stubbing out her cigarette and leaving him alone in the back seat of the car.

He'd asked her where she was going, and she'd told him to shut up and stay there. He was cold and scared, but he'd known better than to complain. They were supposed to be at the grocery store, but he'd seen his mama kissing a man as she went inside the small house.

What the hell? He was shaking like a rookie on his first bull. Mark wiped the sweat off his upper lip with his sleeve. Audrey had better not be sneaking around with Pete. If she were, it'd kill him. He didn't want to think about why. But a small voice said it was because he had started to trust her.

The hell he had! He'd never trust any woman.

Good thing the scrawny kid was leaving tomorrow. He'd have a little talk with the punk and make sure he left tonight. And if he knew what was good for him, he'd never come back.

And tomorrow morning, Mark would put the rest of his plan into action.

Seven

Mark got up early Sunday morning and cornered John and Dalt in the stables, feeding the horses. "Hey, John. Thought maybe we'd have a picnic today."

John's mouth hung open as he dropped the scoop of oats and stared at Mark.

Mark scowled. "What?"

"You're catching flies, John," Dalt said.

John closed his mouth. "You wanna go on a picnic?"

"Roundup's over." Mark shrugged. "Thought we'd take a break. Could you invite Helen? I'll bring the food."

"Uh, sure."

"Thanks." Mark slapped him on the back and headed toward the house.

* * *

"Good morning, Audrey."

Audrey stumbled, and grabbed the banister to stop a potentially dangerous fall down the stairs.

Mark raced up the stairs to catch her. "Be careful!" he snapped as he slid his arm around her waist, holding her snugly against him.

For the past two weeks she'd made her way downstairs at this ungodly hour without one misstep. Even the shock of being addressed by Mark at this time of the morning didn't account for her clumsiness. It was the sexy, seductive tone oozing from those little words. He may have said, "Good morning," but to Audrey it had sounded more like, "I want you."

No, she must be imagining things. She was still half asleep, hearing what she wanted to hear, the words she heard in her dreams.

Turning to look at him was a mistake. He'd lowered his head close to hers, and their mouths were only inches apart. He'd already shaved, and his musky cologne filled her nostrils, sending waves of heat through her body to pool between her thighs. How was she supposed to be careful when his hand on her waist made her incapable of logical thought?

"Thank you," she whispered when they reached the bottom.

Mark's gaze lingered on her lips. She wanted to lean close and press them to his.

"We're goin' on a picnic. Be ready to leave by noon," he said in a raspy voice.

Audrey's heart filled with dread. She should leave now, call Mr. Burke and straighten things out.

She could turn in her story, get her promotion and get

on with her life. Mark couldn't possibly be interested in someone like her. He probably knew who she was, and was playing some cruel game. If she stayed she'd only get hurt. "I can't. Y'all go on."

"Of course you can. It's all been arranged."

He looked so earnest, a hint of something in his eyes. Imploring? Well, why not?

You know why not, Audrey. The longer you stay, the greater the chance he'll discover why you came here. And the harder it will be to leave, her heart whispered.

But the thought tempted her. One more day. One day to pretend. She'd treasure this last day with him. As long as she remembered it was only make-believe.

She exhaled loudly. "All right."

At exactly twelve o'clock, John and Helen rode up to the back porch. Mark rode behind them on Lone Star, leading a dappled gray mare. Wearing the usual jeans and boots, his black cowboy hat pulled low over his forehead, Mark made a commanding and compelling figure.

"Oh, she's beautiful." Audrey approached the gray, crooning soothing words. She held her hand out slowly, and then stroked the mare's nose. "Isn't anybody else coming?" she asked Helen.

"Most of them left this morning. Jim took Ruth into Tyler, and I don't know where Dalt went. Guess it's just us," Helen answered with a wink.

Audrey took the reins to lead the mare to the mounting block by the corral, but Mark came up behind her and leaned close, extending his arm to rub the mare's neck.

His chest brushed against Audrey's shoulder as he whispered in her ear. "Her name's Starlight. She's gentle as a lamb." Grabbing Audrey around the waist, he lifted her up to the saddle. "Swing your right leg over."

"Oh, you don't have to do that!" Audrey protested. She struggled to be let down, but she might as well have been fighting a machine.

"Damn it, swing your leg over!"

After she'd complied and settled into the saddle, she looked down.

Mark glared at her, his hands on his hips. "What the hell was that about?"

"I'm, um, I've always been… I'm too heavy."

"Too heavy for a cripple like me, you mean."

How could he even think that? "No! I mean too heavy for anyone!" She looked away. "I'm fat, okay? I just didn't want you to strain your back."

Mark stepped back. "Darlin', don't you know you're just perfect?"

He sounded so sincere. Did he honestly not see how big her butt and thighs looked in her jeans?

She shouldn't have come today. Her heart ached just being near Mark. This was her last day with him, and now she'd insulted him.

"We're burnin' daylight, folks," John broke in.

Mark shot her a glance before mounting Lone Star, and they set out across the west field.

The warm sun combined with the cool breeze to produce perfect weather. Mark was right about Starlight. The mare responded beautifully and had a smooth gait. Audrey had always loved horses. Her father had made sure all his girls could ride.

Mark cantered up next to Audrey. "I'm gonna have to buy you some boots, woman." He grimaced at her sneakers.

"Mark, I told you—I'm not staying. Thank you for the offer, but I—"

"If you think," he began, his voice lowered, his tone threatening but promising, too, "I'll let you go now, you'd better think again, darlin'."

She had to stop herself from calling to Helen and John, who had ridden ahead.

She desperately searched for something, anything, to divert the conversation. "So, you've probably traveled everywhere on the rodeo circuit. What's your favorite place to visit? I've always wanted to see the Rocky Mountains."

He held her gaze captive, controlling his stallion with the ease of an expert. He was quiet for so long she didn't think he would answer. Finally, he shrugged and looked thoughtful as he said, "Yeah, the Rockies are beautiful, especially in Canada. But I guess my favorite place is the Grand Canyon. You just can't imagine how big it is until you're standing on the edge and looking out. You feel so insignificant. Like you're only a drop of rain in the whole big ocean, you know? And what you do on this earth doesn't really matter."

She had a hard time concealing her astonishment. She'd expected a sightseeing conversation, not philosophy. Intrigued, she asked, "Do you really think what you do doesn't matter?"

He shot her a brief, panic-stricken look, and sidestepped the question with one of his own. "What about you? Have you always lived in Dallas?"

She blinked and paused before answering. She could take a hint. There'd be no soul sharing today—or any day.

"I grew up in Fort Worth. My dad owns a horse farm. Mom used to take us downtown for lunch, and we'd play at the Water Gardens. You've been there before, haven't you?"

"No."

Again, she was shocked. He'd grown up in Fort Worth and never been to the Water Gardens? She longed to ask him about his childhood, but she knew he'd avoid any personal questions.

So she told him all about her family: her mother dying of breast cancer at thirty-nine, leaving Audrey at fourteen to help care for her two younger sisters, Claire and Miranda; her brother-in-law's illness; and her nephew, Devon, who was three. And finally she talked of her daddy, the champion bronc rider.

"My God! You're Glenn Tyson's daughter?"

He was frowning. Why should that bother him? "Do you know him?"

Mark nodded, then looked away, silent.

They finally came to the creek, and Audrey gazed in awe at what had to be one of the most beautiful sights in the world. The vast meadow in front of them was covered with a dense blanket of bluebonnets. The color reminded her of the deep sapphire blue of Mark's eyes. Audrey sat reverently, stunned and speechless at the splendor before her.

John broke the spell. "Well, I don't know about y'all, but my stomach thinks my throat's been cut!"

Helen chuckled and rolled her eyes. "Leave it to John to think of food at a time like this."

John helped Helen dismount, and with a face of stone, Mark helped Audrey. The men took care of the horses while Audrey helped Helen unpack the food and spread the blankets under an old, gnarled oak tree close to the creek.

Audrey tried to ignore Mark as he lowered himself to the ground with a grimace. He and John discussed the beef market while Helen told Audrey about her son and grandkids, who lived in California.

After the meal, John stood, held his hand out to Helen and asked, "Helen, my love, would you care to take a stroll with me along the banks?"

In an exaggerated southern accent, Helen replied, "Why suh. Ah thought you'd nevah ask!" John pulled her to her feet and they walked hand in hand toward the creek.

Mark cursed silently and vowed to kill John for leaving him alone with Audrey. Earlier, he'd have given John a raise for thinking of such a ploy, but he'd just discovered that she wasn't just Audrey, she was Glenn Tyson's daughter.

The afternoon had been torturous bliss. Spending time with Audrey, watching the sunlight play in her hair as the breeze blew wisps of it across her cheek. The way her face lit up when she smiled at him, and hearing her infectious laughter when she described her nephew's antics. He'd admired the love and concern in her voice when she talked of her family, especially her brother-in-law.

Every time he glanced at her shapely legs spread around the horse, he pictured them wrapped around his hips as he plunged into her. But how could he seduce his hero's daughter?

He decided to stand up to put some distance between him and temptation. But getting to his feet was easier said than done. Aware of how awkward he would look trying to stand, he put plan B into action. He lay down, pulled his hat over his eyes, and stuck his hands behind his head.

Irritated at Mark's rudeness, Audrey barely resisted the urge to dump a glass of iced tea on his chest. Of course, if his cotton shirt was wet, it would only make it harder to resist staring at all those hard planes and slopes. He'd rolled up his sleeves, and his biceps bulged as he stretched his arms above his head. She lost her fight with temptation as her gaze traveled down to his concave stomach, and even farther to the other bulge beneath his zippered jeans.

Mercy! It sure was hot for April. Audrey had to pull her blouse away at the neckline and use it to fan her heated face.

She must've sighed out loud. Mark removed his hat and trained his blue eyes on her. She expected a comment, but he only looked at her in stony silence.

It was times like these she wished she was more witty. But he had the power to render her speechless.

He rose up on one elbow to face her. "You ever been to the Grand Canyon?" he asked.

This time, she didn't bother to hide her surprise. She'd thought they'd spend the rest of the afternoon in silence. "No. But I'd love to see it someday. I guess it would probably make me feel insignificant, too."

"Not you." His gaze bored into her.

"Why do you say that? I'm nobody. You've done so much with your life. Think of all the children you've helped with your Stay in School campaign, and all the happy memories you gave to kids who wouldn't normally get to go to the rodeo and meet a celebrity like you." The words gushed from her mouth before she could stop them.

His lip curled in a sneer. "I'm no hero. I needed the tax deductions."

"I don't believe that. I used to dre—"

When she didn't continue, he glanced up sharply and prodded, "You used to dream what?"

She couldn't believe she'd almost told him about her youthful crush. Since she couldn't make herself magically disappear, she decided her best bet was to make something up. "I used to dream of, um, flying on an airplane to anywhere. Tell me more about traveling."

He stared at her a moment. She could tell he debated

whether to believe her or not. Finally, he looked past her into the distance, as if he were seeing a different vista.

He talked of Calgary and Vegas, Tucson and Tulsa. He described the mountains and the deep banks of snow in Canada, the endangered tundra of Alaska and the tall red-woods of California. He lay back as he spoke, waving his arms and using his hands to depict certain images.

Lost in his beautiful portrayal of the places she'd always wanted to see, Audrey lay down, too. Getting comfortable, she rolled over to lie on her side, bending one elbow to hold her head in her hand. Her other hand sifted through the new spring grass and dry pine needles past the blanket's edge.

As his voice died away, she became conscious of how close they were. She lay beside him, only a few inches separating their upper bodies. Their gazes locked and held. His breathing grew heavy. His eyes darkened. He looked like a starving man peering through the window at a feast.

Without thinking, she brought her hand to his cheek and caressed the rough texture with her fingertips.

Mark closed his eyes and turned his face into her hand.

Encouraged to risk more, she smoothed his brow and raked her fingers through the hair at his temple.

He let out a low groan and turned to face her again. Opening his eyes, he whispered, "Audrey."

Tentatively, he reached up and tucked a strand of hair behind her ear. His hand dropped to her shoulder and pulled her to him. Gripping the back of her head, he brought her lips to his. A brief touch, a gentle pressure, then he pulled her closer for a deeper joining. When she didn't resist, he wrapped his arms around her, crushing her chest to his.

While he plundered her mouth, he ran his hands down her back to her bottom, to squeeze and caress. She moaned, and combed her fingers through his hair, releasing the passion she'd saved all these years for him. Her other hand slid down to find his racing heartbeat.

He rolled her beneath him, flattening his body against hers. Deepening the kiss, he pushed his tongue in and out, playing hide-and-seek with hers. He groaned into her mouth, palming her breast, unbuttoning her blouse.

"Audrey," he whispered as he kissed down her neck. "I want you."

"Yes," she whispered back, pulling his shirt from his jeans. She wouldn't stop him this time.

Gathering her breasts in his hands, he nuzzled his face between them, kissing to the edge of her bra. His fingers tugged her bra down, and he covered a nipple with his mouth.

She gasped and he jerked back. But she grasped the back of his head to bring his mouth back. He groaned louder and sucked. She shuddered at the intimate contact, and he moved his mouth over and gave equal attention to the other nipple.

"You feel so good," he said in a strangled voice, bringing his mouth up to hers again. His kiss was fierce and hard. Hands trembling, he raised them to either side of her face. He pulled back, breathing hard, and looked into her eyes.

"Tonight…" Mark rolled off her, leaving the rest of his sentence unsaid. He sat up, turned away and, breathing heavily, ran a hand over his mouth and through his hair.

Audrey bit off a whimper of frustration. She wanted to reach up and pull him back to her. For a moment, she lay dazed and confused, until she heard the sound of grass rustling, and Helen and John carrying on a loud conversation a dozen yards away. Reality came crashing back. She stood and stumbled a few steps away to adjust her clothing.

Thank goodness they were still hidden by the trees, she

thought, brushing grass and pine needles from her hair and clothes. Once her heart rate and breathing slowed, she was absolutely mortified, not to mention amazed, that she, Audrey Tyson, had lain outside, half-undressed, almost making love to Mark Malone. And he'd said, "Tonight."

But she knew there would be no tonight.

Eight

Mark accompanied Audrey to the back porch in silence, helped her dismount and then took their horses to the stables. His fiery look promised pleasures she wouldn't be here to experience.

Audrey dashed up to her room. She grabbed her cell phone from her purse to call Mr. Burke. Two voice mails, one from him and another from her sister.

"Audrey," her boss had said in the message. "What the hell is this about you staying on as a housekeeper? Have you got the story or not? Call me."

She ignored it for now. She'd call him from the road.

The message from her sister was more frantic. Worried for her brother-in-law, Audrey quickly punched in her sister's number.

"Claire, what's the matter? Is it Danny?"

"He's sick, Audrey. He's got a fever and he won't let

me take him to the hospital. He's so stubborn! But he's going whether he wants to or not. Miranda's out of town and Dad has the flu. I don't want Devon sitting around the hospital all night."

Audrey's nephew was only three. The hospital was definitely not the place for him in the middle of the night. "Of course I'll stay with him. I—I'm still at the ranch. I'll explain later. But I'm leaving now. I'll be there in two hours."

Audrey grabbed her suitcase and overnight bag from the closet and threw them on the bed. She was still mostly packed, but snatched up a few things lying around the room.

As she flew down the stairs, Mark stepped into the entryway, directly in her path.

He folded his arms and scowled. "Where do you think you're going?"

Guilt and worry brought a sting of tears to her eyes. She quickly looked down and squeezed them back. This wasn't about her petty problems anymore. "My brother-in-law is sick. I'm afraid it might be pneumonia. I'm going to take care of my nephew while he's in the hospital."

Before she'd even finished the last sentence, Mark had unfolded his arms and stepped closer, pulling her against him. She could smell the scent of new grass and pine from the heat of his body. "They're in Dallas?"

She nodded against his chest. "Arlington. I—"

"We'll take my jet. Have you there in thirty minutes." He stepped back, still caressing her shoulders. "Leave it to me. I'll get you home." Then he turned and strode to his study.

His jet? After a few seconds, Audrey became aware she still stood in the entryway with her mouth hanging open.

Mark was glad he hadn't gotten around to selling the airplane now. He called his buddy, Jake, who agreed to the last-minute flight and met them at the airstrip along the back forty acres of the ranch. Within ten minutes, they were in the air.

Audrey was quiet. She fidgeted in her seat, but he saw nothing in her eyes except worry. Had a part of him hoped to impress her with his jet? How shallow could he get? Besides, hadn't she proven several times she wasn't interested in his money?

There was a municipal airport in Arlington that turned out to be only a few miles from Audrey's sister's home. Mark had arranged for a limo to pick them up.

At the house, the door was opened by a beautiful woman with long blond hair, a flawless complexion and penetrating violet-blue eyes. He'd never seen blue eyes quite that shade before. She was tall, too thin and sported circles under her eyes darker than some football players. He removed his hat and finger-combed his hair.

She looked at him in confusion until Audrey stepped in and hugged her. "Is Danny all right? I wasn't thinking. We could have met you at the hospital."

Audrey's sister hugged her back, her brows creased. "I didn't want Devon there. You're early. What'd you do, fly?"

Audrey stepped back and gestured to Mark. "Oh, Claire, this is, um…the new job I told you about, he offered to…"

Mark stuck out his right hand. "Mark Malone. Nice to meet you, Claire. And yes, we flew."

Claire's gaze darted to Audrey, but she didn't ask any more questions.

A man in an electric wheelchair rolled up. He couldn't have been older than thirty, and had the look of an athlete who'd stopped working out. But Mark knew this guy had had no choice. His face was pale and his eyes were glassy.

As her sister retreated into the house, Audrey bent down and gave him a big hug and a kiss on the cheek. She put her hands on her hips and flashed an exasperated look. "Are you giving my sister a hard time?"

The brother-in-law nodded and grinned.

Audrey pointed her finger at him. "You better take care of yourself. Us Tyson girls stick together, you know."

Again, her brother-in-law nodded and smiled.

"You don't have to hog every conversation," Audrey teased. "You could let me get a word in every once in a while."

The man slid his eyes over to Mark and raised his brows.

"Oh, I'm sorry. Danny, this is Mark Malone, he gave me a ride." She finally looked at Mark. "Mark, this is my brother-in-law, Danny Grant."

Danny turned his head, grabbed a stick with his mouth and pushed a few buttons on the screen of a machine attached to his chair. A stilted male voice said flatly, "Nice—to—meet—you."

Audrey's sister came back carrying a small boy who was a miniature version of the man in the wheelchair. He had big brown eyes and dark curly hair. Audrey swooped the boy into her arms and raised him above her head. "Devon! Give me a kiss."

He gave her a big smooch on the cheek.

The boy wiggled down and moved to stand before Mark. He fingered Mark's hat and said, "Cowboy?"

Claire chuckled. "Devon loves Cowboys and Indians, Mr. Malone. You, uh, still have your horse?"

"Horsies," the kid squealed.

Mark wanted to squat down to the boy, but knew his leg wouldn't hold him. So he bent at the waist and placed his hat on the kid's head. Man, this kid reminded him of Keith. Then an idea hit him. "I've got lots of horses on my ranch. Would you like to ride one?"

The kid's eyes got wide as he nodded.

Audrey gasped. "That's nice of you to offer. But he'll do better in his own home." Out of the corner of his eye he could see her shaking her head and waving her hands at her sister.

Mark ignored her and appealed to the kid's mom. "He could stay for a few days. Get to see a real ranch, ride a pony…."

Claire said, "So, Audrey's staying on for a while longer?"

"No."

"Yes," Mark said at the same time Audrey denied it. Mark clenched his fists. She wasn't getting away from him that easily.

Claire grinned at him. "Are you sure he wouldn't be an imposition?"

Silently, Audrey glared at her younger sibling.

Man, she was cute when she was mad.

Mark looked Audrey right in the eye and said to her sister, "I wouldn't mind at all. We'd love to have him."

Audrey moved in front of her sister and bent down to Devon with her hands on her knees. "Wouldn't you rather stay here with Aunt Audrey and make popcorn and watch a movie?"

"No! Horsies!" the kid exclaimed.

A rush of triumphant adrenaline hit Mark's veins. Just as when he'd had a good ride. He knew he'd won. "He'll have a good time and I'll keep him safe."

Claire looked down at Audrey and back up at him. "Well, I think it's a great idea." She put her hand on Danny's shoulder. "Devon needs to get away for a few days. I'll go pack him a bag. Danny, take Devon to get his toothbrush, will you?"

The man and the boy wheeled out of the room, and Audrey turned on Mark. "I can't go back!"

"Why not?"

She frowned and looked at the floor. "Well, I— Because I—" she stuttered.

Maybe he should let her go. But there was too much passion between them. Too much left undone. "It's too late. Your nephew's got his heart set on riding a horse."

"Mark!" She grabbed his arm when he turned to leave. His skin burned at her touch.

He stopped and turned back to her.

"I know you can find another housekeeper."

He raised a brow and lifted her cold, trembling hand from his arm, taking it in both of his. "Remember what I said, Audrey. You started this. You wanted me sober." He leaned in, lowered his head. "Now I want you." His lips lingered just above hers.

Her eyes fluttered closed.

"And I'm not letting you go," he breathed into her parted lips. "Not yet."

Mark opened his bleary eyes Monday morning and found a pair of dark eyes peering at him as if he were a strange specimen in a petri dish. What the hell had he been thinking bringing this kid to his ranch? He couldn't be any kid's hero anymore.

"Are we going to ride a pony today?" asked the little boy.

"Uh…not right now." Mark sat up, rubbed his face and ran a hand through his hair. "Go find your aunt Audrey."

An Important Message from the Editors

Dear Reader,

If you'd enjoy reading romance novels with larger print that's easier on your eyes, let us send you TWO FREE HARLEQUIN INTRIGUE® NOVELS in our NEW LARGER-PRINT EDITION. These books are complete and unabridged, but the type is set about 25% bigger to make it easier to read. Look inside for an actual-size sample.

By the way, you'll also get a surprise gift with your two free books!

Pam Powers

Peel off Seal and Place Inside...

THE RIGHT WOMAN

she'd thought she was fine. It took Daniel's words and Brooke's question to make her realize she was far from a full recovery.

She'd made a start with her sister's help and she intended to go forward now. Sarah felt as if she'd been living in a darkened room and some- one had suddenly opened a door, letting in the fresh air and sunshine. She could feel its warmth slowly seeping into the coldest part of her. The feeling was liberating. She realized it was only a small step and she had a long way to go, but she was ready to face life again with Serena and her family behind her.

All too soon, they were saying goodbye and Sarah experienced a moment of sadness for all he years she and Serena had missed. But they ad each other now, and th's what

She held

PRINTED IN THE U.S.A.
Publisher acknowledges the copyright holder of the excerpt from this individual work as follows:
THE RIGHT WOMAN Copyright © 2004 by Linda Warren. All rights reserved.
® and TM are trademarks owned and used by the trademark owner and/or its licensee.

YOURS FREE!
*You'll get a great mystery gift with
your two free larger-print books!*

GET TWO FREE
LARGER-PRINT
BOOKS!

YES! Please send me two free Harlequin Intrigue® romantic suspense novels in the larger-print edition, and my free mystery gift, too. I understand that I am under no obligation to purchase anything, as explained on the back of this insert.

PLACE
FREE GIFTS
SEAL
HERE

199 HDL D4A9   399 HDL D4CA

FIRST NAME

LAST NAME

ADDRESS

APT.#

CITY

STATE/PROV.

ZIP/POSTAL CODE

**Are you a current Harlequin Intrigue® subscriber and want
to receive the larger-print edition?**
Call 1-800-221-5011 today!

▼ **DETACH AND MAIL CARD TODAY!** ▼

(H-ILPP-03/05) © 2004 Harlequin Enterprises Ltd.

The Harlequin Reader Service™ — Here's How It Works:

Accepting your 2 free Harlequin Intrigue® larger-print books and gift places you under no obligation to buy anything. You may keep the books and gift and return the shipping statement marked "cancel." If you do not cancel, about a month later we'll send you 6 additional Harlequin Intrigue larger-print books and bill you just $4.49 each in the U.S., or $5.24 each in Canada, plus 25¢ shipping & handling per book and applicable taxes if any.* That's the complete price and — compared to cover prices of $5.24 each in the U.S. and $6.24 each in Canada — it's quite a bargain! You may cancel at any time, but if you choose to continue, every month we'll send you 6 more books, which you may either purchase at the discount price or return to us and cancel your subscription.

*Terms and prices subject to change without notice. Sales tax applicable in N.Y. Canadian residents will be charged applicable provincial taxes and GST.

The boy stared at him with sad brown eyes. "Yes, sir." He turned to go, his chin lowered, his bottom lip trembling.

Mark felt as if someone had reached inside his chest and squeezed his heart. He remembered Keith looking like that all the time. Aw, hell. "Kid. Wait."

The little boy stopped and turned, his expression still bleak, as if he expected more bad news. "Let's go get you a pony."

The boy lifted his face to Mark. "Really?"

"Yeah, let's see. First, you need the right equipment."

The boy's—Devon's—eyes widened. "Can I have a hat, Mr. Lone?"

"Uh, yeah. And call me Mark."

Three hours later, Mark walked into the kitchen with a new little cowboy. Devon was outfitted in Wranglers, a western shirt, boots and a black hat. He swaggered in like a miniature John Wayne, then ruined the effect when he scampered to Audrey. "Audey! Mark got me a pony! I'm a real cowboy!"

Mark was worn out, but it was worth it to see Audrey smiling at him as if he just roped the moon and stars and laid them at her feet. The way he'd longed for her to smile at him since they'd first met.

Audrey instructed Devon to give Mark a hug and tell him thank-you.

"Thank you," the little boy mumbled, wrapping his arms around Mark's bad leg. What he really wanted was a hug from the kid's aunt.

Before he'd finished the thought, Audrey was in his arms and squeezing him tight, her cheek pressed hard to his chest.

This is where she belonged—in his arms. Yesterday's picnic had been a revelation. He'd never talked so freely about himself with anyone. Or lost control. He'd snapped like stressed barbed wire.

This was becoming more than a game. She'd gotten under his skin. When he saw her hugging her sister and brother-in-law with tears in her eyes, how caring she was with her nephew, it made him think about families. Made him dare to dream about having one.

And that was dangerous.

With a beautiful smile, she looked at him, worship in her eyes, and whispered, "Thank you."

Heaven help him.

Mark's throat tightened. He'd never been the recipient of such gratitude for so little. Unable to stop himself, he swooped down and kissed her, starved for the taste of her soft lips. He kissed her possessively, longing for more.

Audrey pushed away sharply, and he felt as if he'd been doused with ice water. The sound of the kid's high-pitched giggling finally penetrated his passion-numbed consciousness. Confused and uncertain, he stood there as she ushered her nephew upstairs, instructing him to let Mark rest, but rest was the furthest thing from his mind.

He took himself out to the corral to saddle the pony, contemplating the days to come. John rode up just as he was tightening the cinch of the child's saddle. The older man dismounted and ambled over to the corral, hooked a booted foot on the bottom rung of the fence and hung his arms over the top rail. "That nephew of Audrey's sure is a cute little rascal," he called across the corral to Mark. "Gonna teach him to ride?"

Mark cocked a brow. "You might say I was roped into it."

John threw his head back and laughed.

* * *

Audrey made Devon a sandwich for lunch and berated herself for oversleeping. When she hadn't found Devon in his room, she'd feared he was bothering Mark. She'd been amazed when she'd found the note stuck to the refrigerator with a magnet. "Kid and I've gone to town. Mark."

She smiled to herself. She couldn't believe he'd bought Devon a pony. But why was she surprised? He'd always been good to children.

Except he'd looked ill at ease when he'd first come home with Devon, standing by the door, hands in his pockets and hat pushed back. If she hadn't known he'd once brought foster children to his ranch, she would have sworn he was uncomfortable around the little boy.

But when Devon had hugged Mark's bad leg, and he'd put his hand on Devon's shoulder, Audrey's heart had turned a somersault. In that moment she'd known she couldn't pretend it was a leftover crush any longer.

She was madly and deeply in love with Mark Malone.

Nine

Trapped.

With no escape. Audrey rolled her shoulders, trying to ease the tension lodged there.

Mark had taken Devon out to the corral for a lesson, and Audrey spied on them from the kitchen window. Watching Mark hold her nephew on the little pony, she fell more deeply in love with the man. She allowed herself to fantasize that they were married, and Devon was theirs and this was her house.

And that she'd never deceived him.

How pathetic was that?

The phone rang, jarring her from her dismal musings. Claire was calling from the hospital. Danny had a circulatory infection, not pneumonia, thank goodness. Still, he wouldn't be discharged for two or three more days. Until then, Audrey was caught in a hell of her own making.

That night after dinner, she hauled a few kitchen chairs into the den and helped Devon stretch blankets across them. Her nephew wanted to "camp out" in front of the fireplace, as the ranch hands sometimes did. Audrey crawled inside the makeshift tent and refilled the bowl with the last of the popcorn. "After you finish this, it's time for bed."

"Aw, I don't wanna go to bed."

A deep voice answered, "You heard your aunt Audrey. No arguing." Mark bent down, grasped Devon under his arms, tossed him in the air and caught him.

Audrey was mesmerized. Wearing that sleeveless sweatshirt, his biceps were displayed to perfection. What was it about the man's arm muscles that literally weakened her knees? Okay, so it was his muscles, and his lips and his eyes....

And the caring way he treated her nephew.

The boy squealed and giggled. A tender look softened Mark's face as he lowered Devon and ruffled his hair. "Got any popcorn for me?" He tugged on the heavy recliner until it faced the fire, and settled into it as if for a long, cozy stay.

"Tell me a story?" Devon asked, handing Mark the bowl of popcorn.

"All right, but you gotta crawl in your tent and lie down."

Devon scrambled to comply and Mark began. "The first time I saw Lone Star, he was bucking and neighing in a big, fancy corral."

As captivated as the boy, Audrey sat on the floor listening to Mark tell how he'd outbid everyone at the auction with his first-prize money to buy the horse.

When Mark stopped speaking, she looked over at Devon. He was fast asleep. "Guess I better put him to bed."

"He's all right for now. Want some coffee?"

Oh, yes, she thought. And you. For the rest of my life. He started to rise, but she shot up from the floor. "I'll get it," she mumbled as she slipped past him. She needed to put some distance between them.

When Audrey returned, she handed Mark a mug and sank back to the floor beside the tent.

"Thanks." Mark accepted his mug, but didn't drink. He sat on the edge of his chair, watching her, his gaze intense.

Distracted and nervous, she took a sip of her coffee. The hot liquid burned her mouth and she hissed her pain.

Mark bent forward, laid his palm on her cheek and lifted her chin. "You all right?" Gazing at her lips, he ran his thumb gently across them. He lowered his head and touched his lips to hers.

Thoughts of the picnic swirled in her head as his mouth opened and he pressed closer. It would be disastrous to succumb to his seduction. How could she when she'd lied to him? She pulled away and scooted out of reach. "Claire says Danny will be home in a few days, so I'll be taking Devon home first thing Thursday morning."

Mark leaned back with a loud sigh. "We'll take him in the jet."

She made herself meet his gaze. "That's not necessary. But thank you for letting him stay here. He's had such a wonderful time."

Mark gazed at the toddler as she spoke, but his mind seemed far away. "He was really good on the pony. Reminds me of my brother."

A piece of the puzzle snapped into place. The boy in the picture. "You have a brother? What's his name?"

Mark gazed into space, lost in thought. His mouth turned down and his eyes took on a haunted look. "Keith."

She wanted so desperately to know everything about Mark. Would he finally talk about his past? Audrey waited.

He continued, "He'll be twenty-two this month. I remember the time Helen made a cake for his seventh birthday. And after we ate it, John took us to the Stockyards and we got to ride a horse. I was fourteen, and John said I was a natural. That was the day I decided I wanted to own a horse someday."

Helen and John? What about his parents?

"Does Keith live close?"

His jaw clenched tight. "Last I heard." He stood, reached for the poker by the fireplace and started jabbing the solitary log.

Last he heard? About his brother? "What about your mom and dad?"

He spun around abruptly. "They're dead," he said fiercely.

Audrey flinched. "Oh, I'm sorry." It was lame, but she knew from experience there was nothing else to say. She wondered how old he'd been when they died.

Breaking into her thoughts, he turned toward her nephew, his face now an unreadable mask. "We should get him in bed."

Mark picked up Devon, and Audrey tried to take him, but he wouldn't let her. She followed them up the stairs, worried as she watched him slowly climb the steep steps, wondering if it caused him pain.

After getting Devon tucked into bed, she quietly said good-night.

Mark stared at her a minute as they stood in the doorway. She could hear his ragged breathing, but he didn't speak or even attempt a kiss. He just turned and headed back down the stairs.

It scared her to realize she'd wanted him to touch her, had yearned to feel his lips on hers again. With a trembling intake of breath, she knew that when she left on Thursday, she might as well tear out her heart and leave it here at the ranch, crushed on the floor.

Mark grabbed the back of his shirt, pulled it over his head and tossed it on the floor. Why the hell had he mentioned Keith? What had possessed him?

He sat on his bed to tug off his boots. He never talked about his past. Never. But it seemed from the moment she'd arrived, Audrey had bewitched him. He thought about her constantly.

His hands trembled as he stood and carefully unzipped his jeans. Since when had he lost control? Even as he'd carried the kid, and his leg had throbbed, he'd wanted to lean down and kiss her. He shucked off the jeans and stalked to the shower, turning the faucet to cold.

When John and Helen had come wandering back from their walk at the picnic, he thought he'd explode. If he'd been thinking straight, he'd never have started something in the open like that, knowing there wasn't enough time to finish it.

But that was just it—he wasn't thinking straight. He was supposed to be seducing her. Not the other way around, damn it. He'd better be careful, or she'd have him pouring out his whole miserable life story, like some pitiful jerk on one of those stupid talk shows.

He shook his head. Like hell, she would.

When she first heard the phone ringing Tuesday morning, Audrey thought maybe it was Claire calling. She rushed from the laundry room to answer it, hoping it wasn't her boss. She'd left him a voice mail, but hadn't heard back from him.

By the time she got to the kitchen, she heard Helen say into the phone, "Yes, I'll tell her."

As Audrey stood in the doorway, Helen hung up the phone and turned to her. "What's going on, Audrey? That man said he was your boss."

The world turned black at the edges of her vision, and she grabbed the door frame. She just couldn't do this anymore. The strain of living a lie, betraying Mark, had taken its toll. She could never expose Mark behind his back. His adoring fans would just have to keep wondering about his mysterious disappearance from the public eye.

How could she feel so strongly about this place, and its people, in such a short time? And why the heck hadn't she considered that possibility before she'd cooked up this harebrained scheme?

For as long as she could remember, she'd always wanted to be a journalist. But, until recently, she'd never believed in her abilities enough to try and make her dream come true. And now, she wasn't sure she wanted to if this was the price she had to pay. She just didn't have the killer instinct to do this job.

Finally, with a sigh, Audrey said, "He is. He's the editor for *Dallas Today*." She pulled out a chair and plopped down, deciding to come clean with Helen. She was relieved that she could share her burden, like a sinner confessing to a priest, asking forgiveness, hoping for mercy.

She told Helen everything. When she finished, she searched Helen's face for a clue to her fate.

Helen was quiet a moment, but she didn't seem upset. "So you've decided not to write the article? You'll lose your chance for a promotion?"

"I swear, Helen, I couldn't betray Mark. Not now. I'll figure out some other way to become a staff writer."

"Well, then, all we have to do now is tell Mark." She waved a hand as if the whole thing were swept away like the piles of empty beer bottles Audrey had found her first day there.

Audrey cringed at the thought of telling Mark the truth. "I just can't. He'd hate me."

"He'll be madder than a cattle-prodded bull at first, but I bet he could be persuaded to get over it." Helen raised her brows and widened her eyes. "And Jim tells me you're a betting woman."

Audrey could feel her face heat at the memory of that poker game. How had she ever gotten the nerve to do such a thing? Helen couldn't possibly know the whole story.

Helen stood and hugged her. "Tell him, Audrey. You and Mark are overdue for a long talk." She headed for the back door and turned. "I miss being around little ones. Why don't John and I take Devon to the zoo tomorrow?" Her mouth turned up in a secretive smile. "I'll ask him if he wants to come over after dinner and spend the night so we can get an early start."

After lunch, Audrey heard the doorbell and opened the door to a fresh-faced man in his early twenties dressed in jeans and a T-shirt. He had blond hair and wore small, wire-framed glasses.

"Yes?"

He hesitated, brows furrowed in uncertainty. "I'm here to see Mark." He looked past her shoulder, as if she were hiding Mark behind her back.

"He won't be back till this afternoon."

"Yeah, Helen told me. I'll wait. You must be the new housekeeper. Audrey?" He ran a hand through his hair. The gesture was disturbingly familiar.

"Yes. Audrey Tyson. Are you a friend of Mr. Malone's?"

He stood a moment in silence, folded his arms and sighed. "Mark's never mentioned me? I'm Keith Malone, his brother."

Under camouflage of pouring him a glass of tea, Audrey hid her curiosity. Keith looked nothing like his brother. He was shorter, slighter and had lighter hair.

He accepted her offer of a drink and sat at the kitchen table. Keith frowned and looked at the glass of tea he clutched in both hands. "After Mark's accident, I realized I needed to see my brother. But Mark wouldn't let anybody into his hospital room. He wouldn't return my calls. So when Helen told me he'd sobered up, I thought I'd take a chance and just show up."

Audrey didn't know what to say to that, so she remained silent.

He looked through the doorway toward the den. "Helen says you've done wonders for the house. But she didn't mention kids."

Devon was watching cartoons. "No, my nephew just arrived yesterday. Mark was kind enough to let him visit."

Keith looked impressed and surprised at the same time. "She said you've made a big difference around here." He began to tell how John and Helen had been their next-door neighbors in Fort Worth. About how they would play catch with John, and eat Helen's homemade cookies. "I've kept in touch over the years. I talk to Helen every week."

By the time they'd finished a couple of glasses of tea, Keith was so open and friendly, Audrey ventured a question about his parents. "It must have been hard not having a mother or a father." She thought of her own mother dying when she was so young. "How old were you when they died?"

Keith's jaw dropped and his brows rose. "Did Mark tell you that? Our parents aren't dead, Audrey."

Ten

Keith refused to say any more on the subject, except that he needed to talk to Mark. "It's past time. I haven't seen him in years."

Audrey could hardly contain her shock. Keith had only been a kid the last time he'd seen Mark. What would Mark do when he saw Keith here?

Audrey had barely finished the thought when she heard boot steps on the porch, and Mark opened the door, calling for Devon to meet him at the corral for more riding lessons.

He stopped midstride and stared at Keith.

Before anyone could speak, Mark turned and strode out. But not before Audrey saw his face. What little tan he'd acquired this week had paled, and his eyes had widened in—what? It was more than shock. It was the look of a tortured man.

Keith shoved his chair back and raced out the back door

after Mark. Audrey shut her eyes and prayed. She grabbed a brownie and sat at the table, using all her willpower not to go watch what happened from the window. All she could think about was the look of agony on Mark's face.

After several more minutes, Keith stepped into the kitchen, hands in the pockets of his jeans, head hanging. Audrey hesitated, and the silence became awkward. "Would you like a brownie?"

"No, thanks." He paced to the sink and looked out the window. "Would you convince him to talk to me, Audrey?"

Audrey gave an unladylike snort. "You'd be better off asking John or Helen."

Keith turned and leaned against the counter. After a long, considering stare, he shrugged. "Helen seemed to think Mark would listen to you."

She shook her head. "I'm just a housekeeper."

"That's not what Helen says. I'd appreciate it if you'd try. Please?" Keith implored.

How could she say no to that?

She found Mark in the barn, in a stall toward the back, saddling the pony. For a few gutless moments, Audrey considered leaving him to his solitude. Where was that assertiveness she'd been cultivating? What the heck was she supposed to say? Obviously a subtle approach was needed. She stepped forward and grabbed the top of the stall door for courage.

"Why won't you talk to your brother?" Okay, so subtlety wasn't her strong point.

Mark whipped around to gape at her, fury sparking in his eyes. "None of your damned business," he snapped. He went back to buckling the bridle.

Audrey shrugged and lowered her head. "I know. But, he's your brother and he cares about you."

Mark grunted.

"He does! You should hear the way he talked about you." She stepped closer. "Everyone deserves a chance to apologize. Life's too short to hold grudges."

Mark turned and narrowed his eyes at her. "You don't know what you're talking about, Audrey. Just let it go."

She raised her chin and glared at him. "I can't. I think family is important. No matter what he did, he was only a kid, and he wants to work things out now, so—"

"He didn't do anything! I'm the one who let *him* down. I left him there alone to fend for himself." He swung around and pitched his brush against the wall at the far end of the stable. "Damn it! You're worse than a fly at a picnic." He stalked toward her. "Just stay the hell out of it!" He pushed his way past her, marching toward the outer doors.

Late that afternoon, Mark was trying to free a cow from a sinkhole when Keith came loping up on Shadow. Aw, hell. Guess he'd just helped himself to the bay gelding. The frightened cow fought and squirmed, bawling loudly, and Mark returned his attention to the job at hand. He lassoed the cow's neck and tied the other end of the rope around his saddle horn. Shoving his hat down hard on his head, he pulled back on Lone Star's reins. The rope stretched taut as Mark backed up, but the cow slipped on the incline and slid back down.

With a messy splat, Keith jumped knee-deep into the mud hole and pushed on the cow's flank. Without his glasses, and sporting that innocent grin, he looked like the kid Mark remembered from a lifetime ago.

"Damn it, Keith!" He dismounted, jumped into the mud and shoved his little brother away from the cow. "One hard kick could kill you!"

Keith clamped his mouth shut, trudged toward Mark and shoved him hard in the chest. "What do you care?"

Mark landed on his backside. He pushed up from the sticky muck. Keith thought he didn't care? All the emotions from his childhood swept through Mark's body, pulsing in his blood. He charged on Keith, bent and grabbed him around the waist, trying to force him out of the mud. White-hot anger and pure adrenaline surged, giving him the strength to lift Keith and wrestle him to the hard ground. They both landed in a heap at the edge of the hole. Mark raised himself to his hands and knees. He hung his head and squeezed his eyes shut. "I always cared."

Keith rolled to the balls of his feet and grabbed him by the collar. He yanked tight and pressed his nose against Mark's. "I'm okay now. It's over."

Mark stared into his kid brother's solemn eyes. He couldn't believe this self-assured man was the same kid he'd deserted. It felt as if a burden had been lifted from him. Keith was okay. He'd survived, better than Mark had. He wanted to say something to his younger brother, but words escaped him.

Keith scrambled up and extended his hand to Mark, reminding Mark of all the times he'd helped Keith off the ground after a backyard tussle. He'd locked that part of his life away for so long, never admitting how much he missed his little brother. He cleared his throat to dislodge the lump that had formed there, wanting to refuse the hand held out to him. He didn't need it.

But maybe his brother did. He slapped his gloved palm into Keith's.

Keith looked down at himself, covered in sludge, and burst into laughter.

Mark tried to smile, but couldn't seem to make the corners of his mouth turn up.

Smacking the mud off his jeans, Keith turned and grabbed Shadow's reins. "You had a great career."

Mark headed for his horse, which still held the rope taut. He was surprised the mention of those rodeo days didn't bother him. "Let's take care of this cow and head in. I'm starved. Maybe there's some chicken and dumplings from last night."

Keith raised his eyebrows and whistled. "Did Audrey make it? I wonder if she's seeing someone."

Mark spun around and glared at his brother. "She's taken. Find your own."

Keith grinned. "Interesting."

The red haze lifted and Mark blinked a couple of times. He drew in a deep breath and allowed half his mouth to lift in a smirk. "What's your degree in? Psychology?"

That night after dinner, Audrey brewed a fresh pot of coffee and then busied herself with laundry.

Tired from the emotional strain of the past couple of days, she poured herself a cup and went out to the back porch to curl up on the glider and watch the sunset. With Devon spending the night at Helen's, Audrey was alone. The long night stretched before her.

Keith was heading back to Denton tonight. This afternoon, as they'd stepped into the kitchen, Audrey had glimpsed Mark slapping Keith on the back. Keith had grinned from ear to ear. It looked as if they'd worked things out.

She wished it were that easy for her. She'd be leaving

in a couple of days, too. That thought caused a physical ache in her chest. A part of her wanted to confess and throw herself into Mark's arms, begging forgiveness, another part knew he wouldn't grant absolution that easily. It had taken him eleven years to talk with his brother.

The small portion of his past he'd given away yesterday gnawed at her. Why had he been estranged from his brother? And why had he lied about his parents being dead? She didn't care about the article anymore. She just wanted to know.

Keith appeared in the doorway, a mug of coffee in one hand. "I hear you're a pretty good poker player."

Audrey choked on her coffee. "Who told you that?" she asked after she quit gasping.

He made a gesture with his free hand that asked, "Mind if I sit down?" At her nod, he made himself comfortable next to her. After he drained his cup, he continued. "Mark says you distracted him with your, um, your—you had an unfair advantage." Bright patches of red appeared on Keith's cheeks, and he tried in vain to avoid glancing at her chest.

She bit her top lip, trying to keep a straight face. They must have had quite a talk. Finally, she gave in to her laughter. "It didn't help that he was drunk. Anyway, I'd do it again in a heartbeat."

Keith took off his glasses, pulled a perfectly pressed handkerchief from the pocket of his jeans and began cleaning the lenses. "You don't have to justify your actions to me. As far as I'm concerned, anyone who could get Mark to stop drinking and work the ranch again deserves a medal." He leaned over and kissed her gently on the cheek. "Or at least a kiss," he said quietly, his eyes full of admiration and gratitude.

Audrey smiled at him and put her hand on his arm,

wishing she'd had a brother like him. If only he knew how she'd deceived them all, she thought guiltily.

"Well, now, isn't this a cozy little scene?" sneered that deep voice from the doorway.

Eleven

Audrey froze, but Keith slowly stood and put his glasses back on. He either didn't feel the waves of fury coming from Mark, or he chose to ignore them.

"Guess I better be going. I played hooky from my classes today."

"Don't break up the party on my account. First Dalt, then Pete and now you?" Mark said, practically spitting out the words.

"What do you mean, 'First Dalt, then Pete'?" Audrey seethed. "Are you implying that I've—"

"I was just telling Audrey goodbye, fool!" Keith jumped in. "Besides, I don't see any ring on her finger!"

"Hell, a ring never stopped Mom!" Mark roared.

Audrey was stunned. She couldn't speak.

Keith shook his head. "I can tell you right now, Audrey is *not* like Mom!" He relaxed his shoulders, took a step back and grinned. "You've got it bad, don't you? You're jealous as hell!" He laughed. "Lucky for you, I've got a fiancée in Denton." He glanced at his watch. "And if I don't leave now, I won't get to see her tonight."

Mark's features slowly eased from rage to bafflement. "You're getting married? When? Why didn't you tell me before?"

"I should have mentioned it. But I figured you'd try to talk me out of it. Why don't you come up to Denton soon? I want you to meet her." Keith moved to open the back door, but he turned and gave Audrey a quick hug. "Goodbye, Audrey. Sure was nice to meet you."

Mark still looked confused as Keith shoved his shoulder and the brothers disappeared into the kitchen. Audrey heard Keith chuckle, "Boy, you should've seen your face! Women sure can twist up your guts, can't they?"

Mark waved to Keith as he drove off, branding himself an idiot as he headed back to the house. When he'd seen Keith kiss Audrey, his vision had blurred and his heart had started pumping a mile a minute. He'd wanted to throw his own brother out on his butt. Was Keith right? Was he jealous? He'd never been possessive of a woman before.

She wasn't in the kitchen or the living room, and all the lights were out. Well, hell. She must've already gone to bed for the night. Audrey in her bed, writhing in the sheets. The image hardened him instantly.

Climbing the stairs was torture on his leg. It ached worse at night. But this couldn't wait until tomorrow. He'd never get any sleep remembering the hurt he'd caused in her eyes. He had enough guilt on his shoulders.

He knocked decisively on her door.

No answer.

He knocked again, longer and more forcefully.

Still no answer.

"Audrey, can we talk for a minute, please?" he asked in a calm and reasonable voice.

"Go. Away."

"We need to discuss this. Open the door," he commanded.

"Just go away. I don't want to talk to you."

"If you don't open this door, I'm gonna kick it in!"

The door jerked open and Audrey spoke through gritted teeth. "What?"

Mark was speechless as his gaze swept over her.

She must've just brushed her long hair. It fell in soft waves past her shoulders, glossy and golden. Seeing her in a plain, white cotton gown started an ache in his gut. And this was no ulcer. The sleeveless gown buttoned down the front from neck to hem, with a modest round neckline. But with her arms crossed, her breasts were pushed together. He wanted to cup his palms around them.

He was ready and at attention.

Audrey looked ready, too. Ready to kill. She glared at him through narrowed eyes. Her beautiful lips were drawn in a tight line.

"Well? I'm listening," she said.

For the life of him he couldn't remember what he'd wanted to say. *Think, Malone!* "I, uh…" He ran his hand over his mouth and down his jaw. "I'm sorry." He swallowed hard and tried to look appropriately ashamed.

If possible, she looked even madder. "Apology not accepted." She shut the door in his face.

Mark stopped the door with the flat of his hand and pushed his way into her room. "Damn it, Audrey, you've gotta listen to me. I know I was an ass, but—"

"Glad we can agree on something. Now get out!" Her

voice was wobbly and stringent at the same time. She pointed at the hallway, and he could see the shadow of her dark nipples through the thin cotton gown.

He couldn't think. He couldn't counterattack. With those weapons at her disposal, he might as well concede defeat. Although, he could handle a lifetime of losing arguments if she always wore that gown when they fought.

Wait a minute, Malone. Lifetime?

Mark was, once again, temporarily speechless. All he wanted right now was to wrap her in his arms and kiss her until all that anger turned to passion. He stepped up to her, slipped his arms around her back and pulled her to him.

Audrey wished she'd never opened that damn door. She resisted, pushing her fists against his chest.

He let out a deep breath and looked into her eyes. "Keith was right. I was a stupid fool tonight."

She twisted away. "Even if your assumptions were true, it's none of your business."

Mark's usual scowl returned as he crossed his arms. "But they aren't true, are they?"

She tilted her head. "Maybe. Maybe not."

In the blink of an eye, he moved in and grabbed her shoulders. "You're not like that. Tell me you're not!"

The misery in his eyes melted the last of her indignation. She sighed. "I'm not sleeping with anyone, okay? I don't know why you would think that, anyway."

Mark raised his head, looking away. "Women aren't generally a real faithful breed."

Audrey stepped away. "You can't lump all women into the same category. Can you imagine Helen ever cheating on John?"

He shrugged. "She's the exception that proves the rule." His eyes flared as if a new thought had just struck him. He looked back down at her. "And you." His gaze fled hers again. "But most women? They like variety. My mother couldn't have stuck to one man if she'd been super-glued to his butt."

The bitterness in his tone made her wince. "Your mother cheated on your dad? Is that why you lied about your parents being dead? They're divorced?"

He didn't answer, and an expression she'd never seen on him crossed his face. Uncertainty.

Shaking his head, he gazed over her shoulder. "I…don't know. They're dead to me."

How could he not know? What had happened to his family? But her questions were drowned out by the thumping of her heart as Mark leaned down and gently kissed her, his lips lingering as if he couldn't bear to break away. Tightening his arms around her, he lowered his head and whispered into her ear, "Let me stay tonight, Audrey."

She hesitated, her mind in turmoil. *He doesn't love you. You've got to stop torturing yourself, go home and get over it.*

But what about all those lonely nights she'd spent at home, wishing…?

How many more lonely nights would she lie awake and regret not making love with Mark Malone? Her cowardice would haunt her forever. She had to risk herself.

Burying her nose in his chest, she said, "Okay."

Mark caught her chin in his hand and tilted her face up. "You're sure?" The hesitancy in his voice made her sure.

She raised her eyes to his and smiled. "Yes."

His blue eyes darkened. He circled his arms under her bottom and lifted her against his chest. "Kiss me, Audrey."

She wrapped her arms around his neck, held captive by the heat in his gaze. Waves of desire coursed through her so powerfully she forgot to worry about her weight as she parted her lips over his.

With a low moan, he consumed her with the strength of a man possessed. One hand slid under her hair, caressing the back of her neck as he angled her head to deepen the kiss. Licks of fire blazed between her thighs as he drove his tongue in and swirled it around the cavern of her mouth.

Pulling back, he hitched her higher and buried his face between her breasts. "God, I love the way you smell."

Her nipples hardened and ached as he nuzzled each breast, leaving damp patches on her gown. "I want to see you, Audrey."

Before she realized his intent, he let her body slide down, raising her gown along the way. He reached for the hem and began to lift.

No! She snatched it from him.

Mark stilled. His hands remained in midair before he gradually straightened and brought them to his sides.

Oh, God. Couldn't they just crawl under the covers? Or at least turn out the light? Audrey hugged her body and focused on the floor between them.

"Should I leave?"

"No!" She looked up.

Mark's jaw muscle twitched and his eyes had hardened to chips of blue ice.

She frowned. "It's just…you know. I'm not…thin."

His shoulders relaxed, his features softened. He took a step closer, bringing two fingers up to tuck a curl behind her ear. "You're perfect." He lowered his lips to her cheek, pressing gentle kisses down her jaw and throat.

Audrey closed her eyes and breathed in his musky scent. Relief swept through her. He was going to stay.

Before she could do more than whimper, he stepped

back, brought toe to heel and pushed off his boots. He kicked them aside, pulled his shirt from his jeans and un-snapped the front.

Then he waited.

A thrill shot through her as she realized he was hers to touch and caress. She brought her trembling fingers to touch his hard chest, running her hands through his soft, chestnut curls. There was a long, vertical scar across his collarbone, and a small, crescent-shaped scar several inches below his right nipple. He must have had a couple other dangerous encounters with bulls over the years. When she leaned in and kissed them, he shivered. She reached to tug his shirt off his shoulders, and he helped her pull his arms from the sleeves. He tossed it on the carpet and said, "Now you."

Oh, Lord. He was so beautiful, so chiseled. There wasn't an ounce of fat on him. Could she do this? As if in slow motion, she forced her hands to unbutton her gown.

His heated gaze followed each tiny button, while his hands clenched at his sides.

She stopped at the fifth button, just below her breasts, her fingers hovering at the edges.

Mark reached for her bodice and spread it wide to gaze hungrily at her breasts. He reached inside and lifted her breasts in his palms, kneading them reverently, his thumbs grazing her puckered nipples, tightening them into aching peaks.

"So beautiful." A growl rumbled in his throat as he low-ered his head and drew one into his mouth. His tongue flicked, and a sharp ache surged between her legs, so in-tense it was painful. She clutched at his hair and moaned. Catching her around the waist, he opened his mouth over her breasts, nibbling and then devouring.

Her knees gave way, and he lifted her in his arms and carried her to the bed. A vague thought formed that she was too heavy and should protest, but she was beyond coherent speech.

Lying beside her, he slid her gown off her shoulders and hugged her to him, kissing her while he rubbed his chest across her lush breasts. He took her hand and pressed it to the long length beneath his zipper. "Touch me. Feel what you do to me."

Hesitantly, Audrey slid her palm up and down his straining hardness. She gazed at his shape, enthralled with the feel of him. When he didn't stop her, she began to explore farther down, and then back up to squeeze the tip.

He growled. "That's enough." He rolled and braced himself above her, crushing her mouth with his. Audrey tensed when he pushed his knee between her legs. "It's all right." He slipped his callused hand under her gown and spread her thighs. His touch burned along her thigh, and then pleasured her where she ached the most.

Audrey squirmed beneath him, pushing into his hand, needing more, striving for something she couldn't quite describe.

He deepened the kiss, entwining his tongue with hers. His fingers seemed to know exactly what she wanted. Blood pounded in her temples and the room spun. Her muscles tightened, and she gasped and clutched him around his waist. "Mark!"

Mark pressed his hard length into her hip, willing himself to be patient. A woman's enjoyment was usually a matter of pride to him, but with Audrey, her pleasure increased his own. He enjoyed watching her uninhibited response as her eyes squeezed shut and her back arched. He cupped her face and softly raked his fingers through her golden tresses.

When her lids fluttered open, he reveled in the fire he'd ignited in her green eyes.

"That was…amazing," she whispered.

He took possession of her mouth, wanting to taste her joy. She tore her lips from his and pulled back to breathe deeply. "I want you inside me. Now. Please, Mark."

"Oh, yes," he breathed into the hollow between her shoulder and neck. She whimpered, and wiggled her luscious body, driving him to the brink. He rose to his forearms and looked into her eyes. "I can't go slow now."

She smiled. "It's all right."

He grappled for an old packet from his wallet and yanked his jeans open. Then he remembered. His damn leg! He couldn't pull his jeans off without some awkward maneuvering. Besides, seeing that grotesque mass of scars would send her running for the door.

Frustrated beyond endurance, he shoved his jeans and underwear to his knees and pushed into her with one long, driving force.

She yelped in pain and stiffened under him, her eyes wide. He stilled.

Clenching his teeth, he forced himself not to move. This was her first time? Why the hell hadn't she said something? No woman her age was still a virgin.

Except Audrey.

Fighting for control, Mark gently pushed her bangs off her forehead. "I'm sorry. Are you okay?"

"I'm all right." She lifted her head and gently kissed his lips and cheeks and eyes. Spreading soft kisses down his jaw and over to his ear, she tugged on the lobe with a gentle bite.

He pulled out and thrust again and again. The feel of

her tight heat surrounding him shattered his control. Sliding his arm beneath her hips, he pushed her into the mattress, groaning as he plunged in to the hilt one last time. His body tightened, and he set his jaw, but a strangled cry escaped as intense pleasure overtook him.

Breathing heavily, he collapsed, burying his face in her neck. Lemon, mixed with the scent of their lovemaking, filled his nostrils. He shivered, exhaling. He knew he should move, but he couldn't make himself leave just yet. He wanted to stay inside her, cushioned on her soft body just a little longer.

Sated, he slid his hips over and drifted into a deep, lethargic sleep. Just as oblivion claimed him, he heard her whisper, "I love you."

Audrey lay awake, holding Mark and reliving every sensual moment. The fingers of one hand combed through the silky curls at his nape, and the other gently stroked the now relaxed muscles of his back. Even her most romantic fantasies couldn't compare to the reality of tonight.

She committed to memory the taste of his salty skin as she'd kissed his beard-roughened jaw. The feel of his muscles tensing, his back slick with sweat as she ran her hands over him. His tongue teasing her nipples. She loved the feeling of being filled by him, of holding him inside her. Of hearing his hoarse groan and seeing that vein in his neck stand out as he'd pushed into her one last time.

Mark snored softly into her neck, still holding her breast. Glancing lower, she grinned. His jeans were gathered around his knees. She stifled the urge to giggle. Maybe she should wake him to remove them. Her eyelids grew heavy, and she, too, drifted into a contented sleep.

She was awakened by a movement at the bottom of the bed. Why had she left the bedside lamp on? She blinked.

Her legs were gently pushed apart by big, warm hands. Mark! She rose onto her elbows. "What are you doing?"

"Shhh, just relax." He licked the inside of her thigh, kissing and nibbling his way higher. "You should've told me this was your first time, darlin'." Stroking her with his thumb, he ran his fingers through her blond curls. He drew back and whispered, "A true blonde, huh?"

Mark had removed his clothes. Gloriously naked, he crawled up, still under the sheet, trailing kisses along the way. He grabbed the bottom of her gown and pulled it over her head, ignoring her gasp of protest.

Audrey crossed her arms over her body and turned away, staring at the nightstand beside them.

"Move your arms, Audrey." He grabbed her wrists and held them to her sides.

She squeezed her eyes shut and held her breath. Oh, God. If he said something about losing weight, she'd die.

Agonizing seconds later, her eyes shot open as she felt his stubbled cheek rub back and forth over her less-than-flat stomach.

"Your little belly turns me on, babe." He eased up the rest of the way and lowered himself on his forearms above her, cupping her face in his palms. "Audrey, look at me."

She forced herself to raise her eyes to his.

"You're beautiful just the way you are, darlin'," he said.

She looked at the ceiling, and couldn't stop the tears that welled up and rolled down her cheeks.

He gently wiped them away with his thumbs. "Why don't you realize how beautiful you are?"

"Beautiful?" She shook her head. "My sisters are beautiful. I'm the plain one. I guess growing up around Claire and Miranda, I learned to rely on my *personality.*"

He picked up a strand of her hair, rubbed it under his

nose and kissed it. "Your eyes are a gorgeous green that remind me of pastures in spring." He kissed her. "Sexy lips." His hand traveled down to caress her hip, moved up to her waist and stopped at her breast to squeeze. "And you're soft and full, not all bony and sharp like some anorexic model."

No one had ever spoken to her this way. His eyes pleaded with her to believe him, desire smoldering in their cobalt depths. She was almost convinced he actually thought her beautiful. Unable to help herself, she'd whispered her love after she was sure he'd fallen asleep. But this time the urge to say she loved him out loud was so strong she ached with it. She could just picture the look of pity—or worse, amusement—on his face. It was less risky to show him her love.

Audrey wanted to explore *his* body. She pushed at his chest.

He frowned. "What are you doin'?"

"Roll over. It's my turn to kiss you everywhere," she said with more determination than she felt.

Then it happened. His face broke into that glorious smile Audrey had seen that long-ago night when he'd rescued her. For a moment, she couldn't breathe.

Still smiling, he flipped obediently onto his back and put his hands behind his head. "Kiss away, darlin'."

She rose to her knees, forgetting her nakedness, and began with his lips. She opened her mouth and kissed him deeply, smiling at his groan. Despite his protest, she moved her lips to his eyes and the tip of his nose. She nibbled down the line of his jaw to his throat, and ran her hands through his curly chest hair as she kissed his nipples. He gripped the sides of her head.

Moving lower, she kissed his flat, taut stomach, pausing to dip her tongue playfully into his belly button. He moaned again, this time deep in his throat. She traveled farther down and explored with her lips and hands down each muscled thigh to the edge of the sheet.

He tensed, grabbed her hand and guided it to his rigid shaft.

She glanced at his face, afraid she'd hurt his leg, but he only smiled and pressed her fingers tighter. Captivated, she gladly encircled him. She'd never felt anything like it before, so soft and warm, yet so solid and alive. She kissed and licked just the tip of him before he gave a strangled choke and reared up to roll her beneath him.

"No more, Audrey!" he gasped.

He kissed her soundly and then raised his head, looking into her eyes. "I need you again, baby." He grinned. "Let's see if I can last longer than eight seconds this time." He brought his lips back to hers and pushed into her with one long, sensuous stroke.

Audrey felt the pressure building inside her with each thrust. The sharp ache between her legs intensified until his rhythmic pressure pushed her over the edge.

Mark watched with pure male pride as her whole body tightened and she practically bucked him off. But he held on tight and thrust one more time. Burying his face in her neck, he stiffened and stilled, enjoying the lingering sensations. He whispered her name before relaxing against her, exhaling a long sigh.

Before Mark fell asleep, he waited to hear her say that she loved him again. A teardrop hit his forehead. He lifted his head. "Did I hurt you?"

She smiled and tightened her arms around his neck. "No. It's just that, you *smiled!*"

He shook his head, puzzled. "You say that like it was some miraculous event. My smilin' makes you cry?"

She chuckled, and rolled her eyes at him, pushing his head back onto her shoulder. "Oh, never mind." She gave a big sigh as he pulled her close to snuggle.

He laid his head on her chest and drifted off to sleep.

Twelve

The sun was just creeping past the horizon when Audrey slowly opened her eyes. She knew she should get up, shower and start breakfast, but she wasn't ready to step back into reality yet. She wanted this dream to last just a few more minutes. To relish all the details in her mind.

Waking up wrapped in Mark's warm, strong arms, hearing his heartbeat as she lay with her head on his chest, smelling his unique odor, her naked skin touching his from head to toe, was true bliss. She'd remember last night forever. And Mark's beautiful smile.

He stirred beside her and kissed the top of her head. "Mmm, I haven't slept this good since I quit drinkin'," he mumbled.

I guess that was kind of romantic.

"I wish I didn't have to get up. I love lyin' in your arms, darlin'." He rolled her over and kissed her thoroughly.

Now, that was more like it! She met his tongue with her own and heard him moan softly. His male scent, his hard body, even the rough scratch of his morning stubble, intensified the ache of all her lonely mornings to come.

"I want you," he whispered into her throat.

"Mmm, I really should get breakfast started." But she said it halfheartedly, even as she wrapped her legs over his. A twinge of pain shot through her thigh muscles. She was sore in places this morning she didn't know a person could be sore in, but it didn't stop her from wanting him again. Did Mark's bad leg ache, too?

Mark groaned and slipped inside her.

One more time, then he really would have to get going. He'd loved waking up with her draped across his chest, her breasts pressed against him. He could spend all day with her in his arms, even if his leg was cramping up. She ran her fingers through his hair and down his back, and he had to suppress the urge to push into her hand like a cat craving a rub.

"Mark, is this hurting your leg?"

Mark stilled in midthrust. Why had she asked him that? Had he favored his injured leg last night and not realized it? Was she feeling sorry for the poor crip? Trying to get a glimpse of the freak's mutilated leg? No. Audrey wouldn't do that to him.

"Mark?" She sounded worried. "I'm sorry. You don't have to talk about it, okay?"

"Uh, yeah. I mean, no. I—you're right. It's getting late. I've got chores to see to." He refused to look at her as he rolled off and scooted to the edge of the bed. He reached for his underwear and jeans and slipped them on.

He'd completely forgotten about his leg after he'd made love with Audrey. All he'd cared about was tasting her and pleasuring her. Feeling her skin against his. What was the matter with him?

Muttering to himself, he located his shirt and grabbed his boots. As he reached the door, the silence hit him. He turned around and glanced at her.

She looked so beautiful with her hair falling over her shoulders and the sheet outlining her magnificent breasts. He expected anger, screaming, accusations. She was scowling—or trying to. But what he saw in her eyes was pain and embarrassment.

What the hell could he say? *I don't want your pity?* He didn't want to bring it up. Not with Audrey.

"I…uh…"

He cleared his throat and tried again. "I—"

"It's getting late. We've both got a lot to do today." She smiled, but it was a pretty dismal attempt. "So, if you wouldn't mind?" She actually made a little shooing motion with her hand.

She was shooing him out?

He knew she was only trying to save her pride. And who could blame her? He didn't want to leave it like this, but he had no idea what to say. This may have started as a physical need, a mutual attraction, but…she'd said she loved him.

He swallowed. "Audrey, last night was…"

"Yeah, um, me, too. I really need a shower before breakfast."

"Damn it, Audrey!" She was going to hear him out if he had to tape her mouth shut! He strode over to the bed, leaned down and took her face between his hands, forcing her to look at him.

"Just listen a minute! Last night was damn good and— aw, hell!" He grabbed her shoulders, pulled her up to her knees and took her mouth in a deep, passionate kiss.

Straightening slowly, he headed for the door. "I'll see you this afternoon."

When he turned back to look at her, she stared at him, her brow creased in confusion.

Mark's leg throbbed all day. Driving the tractor probably didn't help, but, as with riding Lone Star, he had something to prove. And his leg wasn't the only thing throbbing.

Right after dinner, he'd get things straight with Audrey. He couldn't keep his mind on work. Visions of last night brought phantom twinges of pleasure coursing through his body. Just thinking about her made his heart speed up. How perfect they'd been together. He'd never had a woman fill his thoughts so completely. He smiled as he remembered her whispered confession.

She'd said he didn't have to talk about his leg. So he wouldn't. He had some paperwork he really ought to finish, but to hell with that. He'd take Audrey to his room and make sure she was too occupied to think about anything but pleasure.

He ached to be with her right now. He didn't know when or how she'd become so important to him. She was interfering and stubborn and, damn it, he liked her that way! He grinned remembering how she'd poured his beer down the sink. And he'd been her first lover! His throat tightened up. He should feel guilty that she'd wasted her virginity on him. But he didn't. He reveled in the fact that she hadn't slept around.

Yet.

The thought of Audrey being with another man made him feel sick. But it was inevitable. The best he could hope for was a couple of weeks. Maybe a month. Would she stay that long?

He hoped so.

If someone had told him a couple of weeks ago that he'd want more than a good time with a woman, he'd have thought they'd landed on their head once too often. But now, he longed for it. Someone who wanted him, thought she loved him. Course, she didn't really love him, Mark Malone. She loved the *Lone Cowboy*. The legend. The hero. But he might as well enjoy it while it lasted.

"Mark! Watch out!" Jim shouted from his horse. He waved his hat in Mark's face as if he was hazing a calf.

Mark braked with his left foot, pulled his bandanna from his pocket and wiped his face. He'd almost run into Jim.

"You looked like you were in another world for a minute there. Still worried about the drought?"

"Uh, yeah." What else could he say? *No, I was dreaming of how Audrey's beautiful breasts overflow my palms.*

"Want me to finish up here?" Jim offered.

Mark realized he was rubbing his leg. He straightened and adjusted his hat. "No. See you back at the house."

"Nice meeting your brother yesterday." Jim turned his horse to ride away.

Mark nodded. Was it only yesterday he'd quarreled with Keith? Only last night he'd made Audrey his? Each incident seemed like a lifetime ago.

He shook himself. What was he doing sitting here mooning over the woman like a lovesick fool? The blazing afternoon sun must have given him heatstroke. He put the tractor in gear and tried to concentrate on planting grass seed.

With Devon gone for the day Audrey completed her tasks by rote, her mind lost in sensual memories and her heart crumbling like the top on the Dutch apple pie she'd prepared that day.

You will not cry, Audrey Alyse Tyson! You knew how it would be when you made your decision. You wanted the "experience," remember? And what an experience it had been.

She snapped green beans and heaved a big sigh. Making love with Mark was worth it. Even if the pain did equal the pleasure. For a little while, he'd been her magic mirror, reflecting a beautiful, alluring woman.

And she had made him smile!

No, she would never regret last night. She'd known all along that this was just a physical release for him. He probably made every woman he slept with feel special.

Why had she asked him about his leg? That was obviously a touchy subject. But after feeling so close to him last night, she'd longed to know all of him. His past, his dreams, his childhood... What had he said yesterday? Something about leaving Keith to fend for himself? Against whom? His mother? Well, she'd never know. Certainly Mark would never tell her.

That was the painful part—knowing he would never let her get really close to him. Lovers didn't just have sex; they shared the deepest part of themselves with each other. Or at least that's what Audrey thought they should do. But whenever she'd asked personal questions, he'd pushed her away.

Audrey was leaning into the fridge for lettuce when footsteps sounded behind her. She barely had time to turn before a masculine arm stole around her waist.

It wasn't Mark's arm.

Pete brought his other arm around her back and squeezed the breath from her lungs as he pressed her to him. "I'll show that damn crip he can't scare me off." His fetid breath offended Audrey's nostrils as he leaned over her and forced his mouth over hers. Struggling made no difference. She was cornered against the refrigerator, its door between her and the block of knives.

Finally, he came up for air. "I've been dreamin' of gettin' you naked ever since I saw you."

Audrey sucked in a short breath and turned her head, avoiding his persistent lips. "Pete, I can't breathe."

The minute he loosened his grip behind her back, she shoved hard.

Pete fell back and knocked into the table. His face contorted in rage. "You witch!" he roared, lunging for her throat.

Audrey made a dive to the right, hoping to reach the drawer containing the ice pick.

He captured her arms and pinned them behind her back.

Audrey kicked out behind her, hitting his shin, but Pete only tightened his arm around her waist. He grabbed her hair, yanked her head back and planted his wet lips on her neck. "Don't fight me, Audrey. You won't win."

Mark was still smiling when he drove the tractor into the shed and saw John heading his way.

John greeted him with a nod. "I'm glad you and Keith worked things out."

"Me, too. Hey, did you know he's getting married? I can't believe my little brother's fool enough to ask for that kind of grief." Mark held his hands up and smirked. "Uh, no offense to Helen."

Mark expected John to commiserate, but he gave him a serious look. "Marrying Helen was the best thing I ever did."

Mark shrugged. "I just hope he knows what he's gettin' himself into, that's all."

"What about you? You ever think about taking the bull by the horns?"

"Me? Hell, no!" John might as well have proposed he strip naked and run through the streets of Quitman.

John shook his head. "Well, I'm eatin' with my wife tonight. See you tomorrow."

And Mark was eating dinner with Audrey tonight.

After washing up at the bunkhouse, Mark headed for the kitchen, trying to tamp down his potent anticipation by reminding himself this was only temporary.

As he stepped in the back door, his heart stopped and all thoughts of seduction vanished.

Pete had Audrey cornered between the stove and refrigerator. He had one hand around her throat, the other behind her head, forcing his mouth on hers.

Audrey fought him, yanking on his hair, terror etched on her face.

Rage clouded his vision. He swung Pete around by the shoulder, reared back and punched him in the jaw.

Pete landed hard, several feet away, with a satisfying thud.

Mark wanted to wrap his hands around Pete's scrawny neck! "Get up, you bastard."

Pete stayed on the floor, his palms up. "She asked for it, man."

Mark blinked, clenching his fists to keep from dragging the punk up by his shirt and beating him to a bloody pulp. "I'll give you thirty seconds to get your butt off my property before I call the sheriff. You set foot on this ranch again, I'll make you wish you were dead."

Pete scrambled up, swiping the blood from his nose. He sneered as he kicked open the back door and strode off.

Mark turned to Audrey and she flew into his arms. "Did he hurt you, darlin'?" he whispered, pulling her close and stroking her tangled hair.

She buried her face in his chest. "N-no," she croaked.

Damn, she was shaking. He should have killed the son of a bitch. "I'm sorry, baby. I thought I'd made sure he wouldn't bother you. I'm calling Sheriff Townsend."

She clung to him tighter. "Don't let go!"

Despite his fear and rage, he smiled and moved his arms down her back, caressing, comforting. "I won't." He liked this feeling. Rescuer, protector, lover. She was his, and he'd do anything for her.

Pressed against him, he could feel her trembling breaths and the moisture on his shirt. "You sure you're okay? Where's Devon?"

She nodded, and the movement rubbed his shirt. "He's at the zoo with Helen."

He took her shoulders and leaned back to look into her eyes. "Pete won't bother you again, I promise."

Audrey gave him a wobbly smile and stepped from his arms. "I'm all right now." She moved to the stove, avoiding his gaze. Grabbing a towel, she opened the oven, pulled out a pie and put it on the counter.

Mark put his arms around her waist, brushing her cheek with his lips.

Audrey melted into his embrace. In his arms she was safe. If only she could stay this way forever.

She'd never been attacked before, never felt so threatened. Pete had been so strong. She'd like to think she'd have fought him off eventually, but the truth was, if Mark hadn't shown up, she wasn't sure.

All she knew was Mark had rescued her again, and she loved him, and she'd make love with him right here on the kitchen table if Jim and Dalt weren't due to show up for dinner any minute.

What was she thinking? She had to calm down and remember this morning's resolve. One night was a special memory. Anything more and her hard won self-respect would be chipped away a little each day. He'd tire of her, or find out who she was. She couldn't go there. She moved to start setting the table.

Desire radiated from him as he stalked her across the kitchen. His eyes held a determined glint and his hands flexed at his sides.

She held her hands in front of her in a feeble attempt to ward him off. They met his hard chest, and she could feel his heart beating double-time. He captured her hands and kept them pressed to his chest while he lowered his mouth to hers.

No! She turned her head at the last moment. She'd never let him go if she started kissing him now. "Don't you want to eat?"

"Yeah, I'm starving." He gave her a wicked grin.

His grin immobilized her. She still wasn't used to seeing him smile. She leaned her forehead against his chest. Even his sweat smelled sexy.

He raised his hand to her cheek and lifted her face. "Embarrassed? After last night?" Enfolding her in his powerful arms, he kissed her tenderly. "I know Pete frightened you, but I would never hurt you," he mumbled against her lips.

"Mark."

The next kiss was deeper, possessive. "I've wanted you all day, darlin'."

She pushed against his chest and he loosened his hold. "I don't think this is a good idea."

He stiffened and dropped his arms. "What are you talking about? What's the matter?"

She mustered up her courage and looked him in the eye. That muscle in his jaw was working overtime. She sighed heavily. "Sit down, okay? I need you to listen."

"I don't need to sit down. I am listening."

The sound of the hands' boots stomping on the back porch promptly ended any discussion. Dinnertime. Audrey was relieved, but Mark cursed under his breath as she rushed to put plates and silverware on the table.

Mark crossed his arms in front of his chest. "This isn't over."

After dinner, Mark decided he'd had enough. Audrey acted as if he had mad cow disease. Had Pete scared her that much? She had to know *he'd* never force her.

Mark stalked into the kitchen and grabbed a towel. The sooner the dishes were done, the sooner they could…talk.

But while he was drying the last pot, she slipped past him and out of the kitchen. He followed her and caught her halfway up the stairs. He grabbed her hand and stopped her on the stairs. "Not so fast. You want to explain what you meant earlier?"

"No, not particularly. Devon's waiting for me to tuck him in." She tugged at her hand, but he hauled her to him and held her close.

"I already did. He's fast asleep." He liked her standing a step above him. He didn't have to lean down to capture her mouth. Closing his eyes, he breathed in her lemony scent. "Talk to me, Audrey. Tell me why you don't want this." His lips lingered on hers.

She pushed away from him. "Please, Mark. I can't think when you're this close."

"Good. Don't think." He tightened his arms and brushed his lips over the sexy little spot below her ear.

"Mark, I can't do this."

"Why not?"

"I'm leaving in two days. Let's just forget it."

"Forget, hell!" He took a couple of deep breaths to calm himself.

He was determined to persuade her. After sleeping in her arms last night, his bed would seem lonely without her. He'd meant what he'd said that morning. Peace had filled his soul, and he hadn't slept so deeply since—well, never. He knew he'd rushed things the first time, but he'd made sure she had her pleasure. So what was the problem?

Leaning down, he spoke softly in her ear. "Are you gonna forget how it feels when I'm inside you? How I made you shiver and beg for more? 'Cause I sure as hell can't forget the way your nipples tighten when I kiss you, and the feel of your hands all over me. Just be with me tonight, honey, and quit thinkin' things to death." He licked her lobe and spread gentle kisses down her jaw to her throat, persuading with his lips and tongue.

Audrey lost her breath and her resolve with his sensuous murmurings. His hands pushed her hips into his, and his mouth captured hers. His tongue swept in and out, raising little chill bumps on her arms and behind her neck. She succumbed to Mark's overpowering persuasion. Instead of pushing him away, she whimpered and ran her hands down his chest and around his waist.

He groaned and covered her breast with his palm.

That action brought her back to reality. Somehow, she summoned the strength to tear her mouth away. If she could just resist for one more day, Danny would be home from the hospital.

"No, I can't do this." Pushing away, she headed up the stairs. "Good night, Mark."

He caught up to her on the landing and grabbed her wrist. "What kind of game are you playin'?"

Audrey twisted from his grasp. "This was all a mistake. I'm not who you think I am." She clamped her hands over her mouth.

Tense silence hung in the air. Amazingly, Mark looked more bewildered than suspicious. "What do you mean?"

How could she tell him the truth after last night? What would he think of her? She chickened out, looked at the floor. "Never mind."

"What do you mean, never mind? What the hell are you sayin'?"

She panicked. Her mind scrambled for something to tell him that would scare him off, make him drop it. A half-truth. "Mark, I just can't have an affair. I would want more. I want a home of my own and kids and everything. And you don't want that." Then, piteously hopeful, she added, "Do you?"

Mark looked appalled. "Kids? Hell, no!"

Audrey flinched at his outburst. Had she even dared to hope he would want something permanent with her? He could have the most beautiful women in Texas at his fingertips, probably already had. The humiliation was unbearable, the rejection excruciating. This time he didn't prevent her from retreating to her bedroom…alone.

Thirteen

Audrey leaned against a leafy oak and quietly observed Mark and Devon in the corral. The famous cowboy coached the small boy with calm words and infinite patience. Along with her special night, she folded this precious memory and stored it in her heart to pull out in the years to come.

His large hand gently stroked the pony's nose, and she remembered how it felt sliding over her skin, cupping her breast. She shivered.

Devon laughed and brought her mind back to the present. The little boy held the reins tightly, as Mark taught him how to control the pony with verbal commands.

"Whoa, Little Star," Devon called to the black pony he'd been allowed to name.

"Ready for cookies and lemonade?" Audrey called from the yard. Not that she expected Mark to come in. After last night, things could only be awkward between them. He'd probably avoid her now. She'd known he didn't love her, but that cruel reality didn't stop her heart from breaking.

She hurried back into the house, though she knew they'd be another fifteen minutes or more. Mark would make sure Devon helped rub down and feed Little Star. "A cowboy always takes care of his horse." Devon had solemnly quoted Mark's words to her with a grown-up expression on his small face.

She removed the jug of lemonade from the refrigerator and took some cups from the cabinet. Pulling the tray from the oven, she transferred cookies to a ceramic platter. She heard Mark on the back porch, quietly instructing Devon to wipe his boots. Her stomach did a somersault. Would he join them?

"Aunt Audey, did you see me riding?" Devon shouted as he clambered onto a kitchen chair.

Mark stayed by the door, taking in the beautiful sight of Audrey in a green-checkered apron, pouring glasses of lemonade.

Homemade oatmeal cookies. They smelled good. Seeing the little boy reach for a cookie reminded him of when he and Keith were kids and their Mom would lock them outside. Helen would ask them in and feed them cookies and chocolate milk. He could still picture the terrified look on Keith's face when their mom yelled at them from across the yard to get their butts home.

His stomach ached, but he didn't think eating would help. God, he'd missed Audrey last night. Couldn't sleep for thinking about what she'd said. He'd pictured her with a big, rounded stomach, or nursing a baby. Pictured himself holding a little blond-haired girl who called him "Daddy." For the first time in his life, he'd actually allowed himself to consider the possibility.

But then he'd remembered him and Keith hiding from their mother's wrath, and the belt she used when she caught them. That stopped him cold. No way would he bring a kid into this world. No woman was that trustworthy. Audrey was pretty good with her nephew, but he was temporary. How would she handle a permanent responsibility? More importantly, how would he?

You can't have that, Malone. You can't risk it. A sharp pain sliced through his midsection.

He took off his hat, hung it on a wall peg and wiped his forehead on his sleeve. Then he stepped up to the table and grabbed a cookie from the platter. What was he doing? He should turn around and get the hell out of there. *It's over. You knew that last night. Quit torturing yourself like this.*

But his legs wouldn't move. And he couldn't take his eyes off her.

When Audrey looked at him, he mumbled, "Oatmeal's my favorite."

Her eyes burned into his from across the table. "I know." She dropped her gaze and smoothed her apron over her hips. "Helen told me."

He stood, mesmerized, yearning for her touch, craving a dream. Remembering.

Devon pulled the platter close to him to grab another cookie. It tipped over the edge and crashed to the floor.

"Oh, Devon! No!" Audrey reached for the little boy.

Before she could get to him, Mark scooped him up and held him away from her. "Don't you dare touch him!" he yelled, rage pumping through his veins. "It was just an accident!"

A tense silence hung over the room like a ghostly presence spreading cold and gloom.

Mark blinked as the haze cleared from his eyes. Oh, God. What had he done?

Devon was shaking, his eyes wide and trained on him.

Audrey's brows were crinkled, her eyes filled with bewilderment…and pity. Finally, she said quietly, "I only wanted to get him away from the glass so he wouldn't cut himself."

Mark choked and dragged in a ragged breath, trying to control the trembling that had taken over his body. He set the boy down and turned his back on her, cursing as his mind reeled. He'd made a damn fool of himself. She'd never look at him without pity again.

She was soothing the boy and sending him to the den to watch television. A moment later, she touched Mark's arm.

"Mark, I hope you know I would never, ever, hurt a child."

"Yeah." He couldn't say any more or she'd hear his voice shaking. And he refused to turn around and look at her. Without a backward glance, he slammed out the back door.

Mark didn't return that evening. With a certainty beyond her understanding, Audrey knew she must find him, and she knew exactly what she would say.

After dinner, Audrey sought out Ruth in the bunkhouse. Jim was just coming in. "Can either of you tell me where I might find Mark?"

Ruth shrugged. "Well, there's only two bars—er…" She looked at Jim.

Jim stuck his hands in his jeans pockets and shrugged. "Try the Texas Rose first."

"Will you two watch Devon this evening? I—I need to talk to him."

"Sure." Jim's mischievous grin returned. "I'll teach him to play Go Fish!"

Audrey looked back at Ruth. "Where's Dalt?"

Ruth shrugged. "We were both ready for greener pastures."

Before she left, Audrey settled Devon at the card table in the dining room with Ruth and Jim and then headed out for Helen and John's place. At the last minute, she came back and grabbed Mark's Stetson off the peg in the kitchen.

He wasn't with John and Helen, so she got back in her hatchback and drove into Quitman. It was a small enough town. Hopefully, he hadn't gone into Tyler.

He wasn't at the Texas Rose, either. She found his truck parked in front of Sam's. The place was empty except for a couple of grungy-looking older men in the back. The stench of cigarettes and booze hung thickly in the air, and a television blared from one corner of the ceiling.

She stepped farther in and saw Mark leaning against the bar, hands clenched around a tumbler of golden liquid. A dark lock of hair curled down his forehead. He stared into his glass as if contemplating drowning in it.

Audrey closed her eyes and took a deep breath, then focused her gaze. As she walked toward him, time slowed, her surroundings blurred, her heartbeat thrummed in her ears.

"You forgot your hat." She set his black Stetson on the bar in front of her.

He turned on her, teeth bared like a rabid dog. "Get that out of here."

Audrey forced a swallow past the lump in her throat. She straightened her back and squared her shoulders. "Why?"

Mark shoved the full tumbler across the counter, splashing the alcohol. "I haven't taken a drink, if that's what you're worried about. Save your preaching for someone else."

How long had he been staring at that glass? He must have wanted to drink so badly. But he hadn't. Her eyes stung with tears but she blinked them away. "If you're not drinking anyway, come home with me. I mean…come back to the Double M."

His eyes flared wide and then squinted in menace. "Get the hell out of here before I do something we'll both regret. You better run on back to Dallas, little Miss Innocent."

Audrey smiled and shook her head. "You would never hurt me, or any woman."

His menacing snarl faded into a miserable frown. "What makes you so sure?"

Drawing a deep breath for courage, Audrey said, "Come with me, and I'll tell you."

Agonizing minutes went by while he stared at her. He dropped his gaze and then closed his eyes. "Go away, Audrey." He didn't move or open his eyes. "Please." He spoke the last word on a deep sigh.

"I'm not leaving without you. If you come with me, I'll tell you a secret about me."

His head jerked up and he narrowed his eyes at her. "What? You got a ticket for jaywalking? You voted for Ross Perot?"

She heaved a sigh, pulled up a stool and sat down. "You rescued a young girl once. Do you remember?"

Mark's gaze traveled down her body and back to her eyes. "What?"

Audrey stared at the scarred wooden counter, that long-ago night as vivid as this moment. "You'd just won your first championship. You came into Lone Star's stall. There was a fat girl, cornered by some drunken bullies."

Mark went still. "That was you," he whispered.

She looked into his eyes. "Yes."

"Damn." He lurched away and left the bar, his face creased in bewildered pain.

Tears stung her eyes as she jumped off the stool and followed. She'd hoped to make him see that he wasn't the only one with a painful past. Had she said the wrong thing…again? She pushed out the door.

It was still light, but the sun was almost down and the building cast dark shadows. She could barely see him as he strode down the gravel parking lot. She caught his arm. "Where are you going?"

He yanked away. "Go back to the ranch, Audrey. Don't waste your time. I'm not worth it." He turned and headed for the field behind the bar.

She might not have had the red hair of her father and younger sister, but she had just as much Tyson stubbornness. Setting her jaw, she ran back for his hat and then set out after him.

Even at a brisk pace, it took her a few minutes to catch up to his long stride. When she did, he rounded on her, grabbed her upper arms and shook her.

"I don't need your pity," he said through gritted teeth.

Audrey set her hands at her waist. "Pity? I just told you about the most embarrassing moment in my life, and you walked away. I was trying to tell you how much I admire you. To remind you of all the wonderful—"

Mark cursed, dropped his hands and stalked off across the field.

It was getting dark. Audrey raced after him, grabbed him around the waist from behind and held on tight. "Don't leave."

His chest expanded and Audrey almost lost her grip.

Then he gave a heavy sigh and turned in her arms. He reached behind himself, grabbed the hat from her fingers and flung it across the grassy meadow. As he looked back at her, he grasped her shoulders and gently pushed her away. "It wasn't me that saved you that night."

Shock coursed through her body. "What are you talking about?"

"That was the *Lone Cowboy*. I'd just come off the high of riding that bull and winning that buckle. I could do anything, be anything when I was rodeoing. But that's not who I really am. I tried. I put that hat back on and tried to be him again these last couple of weeks, but I was bound to mess up eventually."

Audrey raised her eyes to the stars sparkling in the night sky, and knew she must take the ultimate risk. She stepped close and put her hands on his chest. "Mark, I don't love the *Lone Cowboy*. I love you."

He gripped her wrists and yanked them away. "You don't know me. I'm no hero."

Audrey framed his face and rose on tiptoe to gently kiss his stubbled cheek, wanting to soothe the anguish she saw blazing in his eyes. "Tell me, then, why I shouldn't love you."

She could feel his jaw clench beneath her palms, and his temples were damp with sweat under her fingertips.

"You're one stubborn woman!" He pulled away and turned his back to her.

She stepped in front of him, but he turned his head and squeezed his eyes shut. "You don't understand. You don't know."

She swallowed. "Then help me understand."

Mark drew in a shuddering breath, his whole body trembling.

Audrey couldn't stand to see him like this. But she remained silent.

"I don't remember my father ever being drunk. So we never had any warning. He was stone-cold sober and, wham, out of the blue, he'd let Mom have it. And then she'd take it out on us. But I had my revenge.

"I was ten when I'd finally had enough. I knew Mom had boyfriends, 'cause she used to take me with her to use as her alibi. Then, I told Dad about Mom's little secret—that he wasn't Keith's real father." Mark stopped and wiped his sleeve across his eyes. He made a choking sound and his hand shook as he rubbed the back of it across his mouth.

"He beat her so bad she was in the hospital for weeks. He went to prison, and I never saw him again."

Oh, Mark. Audrey closed the distance between them and placed her hand on his back. "Mark, you were just a kid. You were too young to understand the consequences."

Audrey gathered him into her arms, but he remained stiff.

"Some hero, huh? You still think you love me?"

Though she couldn't stop the tears that ran down her cheeks, she looked into his eyes with a calm certainty. "Yes, Mark. I love you."

"No." He shook his head.

"I love the man who would never raise his hand to a woman, even when he's got a raging hangover and she pours his beer down the sink.

"I love the man who throws a poker game so a scared virgin won't have to have sex because of a bet."

"How did—"

"I love the man who used his jet to help his housekeeper's sister."

He crushed her to him and kissed the top of her head.

"I love the tender man who bought a little boy a pony and taught him to ride."

Mark groaned as he fell to one knee and pushed her down to the soft bed of grass, ravishing her mouth with a harsh kiss. He couldn't get her shirt off fast enough.

Audrey let him undress her. He needed someone right now. Someone to hold him tight and love him, no matter what.

And she needed him.

He palmed her breasts and sucked each nipple in turn before kissing his way back to her mouth. His lips journeyed frantically down her neck to her breasts again, but soon returned to devour her mouth with a low groan.

With her help, he pulled her jeans off. Audrey held him close and returned his kisses.

Mark freed his rigid member and pushed into her. He couldn't begin to fathom the depths of the longing that threatened to swallow him. He simply let it wash over him as he buried his face in her neck, pumped into her and whispered her name over and over.

With her legs wrapped around him, her hand running through his hair and her scent permeating his nostrils, he was surrounded by Audrey and her love. Keeping the world at bay, he was safe for one moment. For one moment, as his body tightened and his passion spilled out, he couldn't think. He could only feel…soft, safe, free, good, whole, loved.

Fourteen

She loved him. Audrey had said she loved him, Mark Malone. The thought consumed him. She knew the worst of it, and she loved him anyway. She had cried. No woman had ever cried for him.

He rode out to the north pasture, but he knew he wouldn't get any work done today. Devon was leaving, and Mark wished he'd taken the day off and gone with Audrey to take him home. That way, he'd have her all to himself on the plane ride home.

If he hurried, he could still make it. He turned Lone Star around and galloped him home.

When he came into the kitchen, she wasn't there. He stopped in the dining room and saw her standing at the open front door, surrounded by suitcases. Too many just for Devon.

She hugged her nephew and sent him off with Dalt to say goodbye to the pony.

As Mark watched her, his scarred heart took a tumble off a bucking bronc, and the hard shell he'd built around it cracked like the bones he'd broken in his rodeo days. She couldn't leave him now.

He wanted to hold her. After only a few hours, he missed the feel of her in his arms. But he wanted more. He wanted to hear her say she loved him again. Every day. And he wanted to tell her he loved her, too.

Where had that come from? He loved her?

Did he?

Yes, a tiny voice whispered. And he knew it was true.

He watched Audrey wave her nephew off and step away from the front door. "Mr. Burke! What are you doing here?"

Mr. Burke? Who the hell was Mr. Burke?

A hefty man in an expensive suit pushed his way past Audrey and strutted in, looking around. "So this is the *Lone Cowboy*'s house, huh? You better have a good story for the magazine after all this time."

The word *magazine* echoed and pounded into Mark's brain. Something snapped inside him. His chest constricted and he couldn't breathe. She was a reporter? *All she'd ever wanted was a story?* What a fool he'd been, thinking Audrey was different! His stomach cramped. He couldn't see. Must be sweat—it sure as hell wasn't tears—in his eyes.

How she must've been laughing her butt off these past weeks. The pitiful drunk who fell for the little schemer.

"About the article," Audrey began as she closed the front door. She turned to face the pompous man, looked past his shoulder and met Mark's eyes. "Oh, no!"

If she didn't get out of here right now, Mark was going to wrap his hands around her lying neck and strangle her. "Get out!" he yelled. "Both of you! Now!"

Audrey came toward him, her hand outstretched. "Oh, Mark. It's not what you think. Please let me explain. I…I never meant to hurt anyone."

She lifted her hand as if she might touch his arm.

He flinched and jerked away. "Don't."

She was so convincing in her apologetic role. She'd probably rehearsed in case she got caught.

He crossed his arms, making sure he stared at her full-figured hips. "We both got what we wanted."

Audrey recoiled as if she'd been physically slapped, and all the color drained from her face. She swayed as if she might faint, staggering to catch herself.

"Now get out!" Mark yelled.

She didn't even look to see if the man followed her when she raced out the front door, choking on a sob.

Burke—Audrey's boss, he assumed—stared at him.

Mark's fist curled and he took a step toward him.

The man snapped into motion and followed Audrey out.

Mark slammed the door, wiped his eyes and staggered to the recliner. Everything hurt. He dropped to the edge of the chair, doubled over with the pain. He couldn't catch a breath.

Just thinking about his private life being plastered all over the front page of some tabloid made him want a drink. Mark had to warn his brother. And, hell, he'd have to talk to his mother, too. Once the story broke, more reporters would come snooping around.

His mother would enjoy that. She and Audrey ought to get together and compare notes. Start a consulting business on how to be a deceitful shrew.

Maybe he'd sell this ranch, after all. Move to a different state. But first, he had to do what he'd sworn he would never do.

Go home.

* * *

Danny was home, and over the infection. He and Claire were glad to see Devon again, and there were hugs of greeting all around. But Audrey didn't stay long. Telling them she was exhausted, she kissed them all goodbye and drove to her apartment.

She was resigned to whatever her fate might be with the magazine. Her heart was breaking. What was her career compared to that?

Though she'd known it would end eventually, she'd savored the fantasy. Her last night at the Double M had been the sweetest torment. Being in Mark's arms, loving him one last time. They'd clung to each other for a while and then gotten dressed. He'd walked her to her car and driven her back to the ranch, all without saying a word.

She hadn't expected him to return her love. But she hated that he'd discovered her deceit. Now he'd never believe she loved him. A stab of pain hit her heart at that thought.

The next morning, she began her new job dispensing advice to troubled lovers. What a joke. For the first time in her life, Audrey lost her appetite. As diets go, this had to be the most excruciating way to lose weight. Over the next couple of weeks, she had to force herself to eat. Not even chocolate could coax her into caring about her life.

It took all her emotional strength just to wake up and face each day. All she wanted to do was curl up on her couch and stay blessedly numb. She'd come so close to a dream she'd never hoped to live, and deceived a man who had been betrayed once too often.

"Come on, Aud," Miranda cajoled, sitting next to her sister on the couch. "Let's go shopping. Claire's in-laws are in town to watch Devon, and I need a new suit."

After two weeks of her moping around, Audrey's sisters had shown up, determined to coax her out of the blues.

"Audrey, you're pale, you have dark circles under your eyes and your hair looks like a rat's nest. Now get off your butt and take a shower. You're coming with us!"

Three hours and three makeovers later, the sisters sat down in the mall for some frozen yogurt.

"Now." Claire looked determined as she scooped up her yogurt. "Tell us what happened. What happened with the story? Did you get it or not?"

Audrey opened her mouth, but no words would come. How to explain? She realized she'd never shared her feelings with her sisters, believing it was her job to listen and advise, not burden them with her insecurities. Perhaps she wouldn't be in this mess if she'd gone to them in the first place. In that moment, her perception shifted and so did their relationship. She wasn't alone.

"Come on, Audrey. Spill it," Miranda said.

Claire grasped her shoulder, her brows furrowed in concern. "We're really worried about you."

Audrey shook her head. She was so ashamed. "I've ruined everything!" The look on her sisters' faces changed from concern to disbelief as she told them what she'd done.

Claire put her hand over Audrey's. "You love the cowboy?"

Audrey nodded.

Miranda spoke up. "You should be glad you're rid of that redneck. He'd only end up hurting you. Believe me!"

Audrey exchanged a shocked look with Claire. She turned to Miranda, frowning. "Randa, has something happened between you and Ron?"

Miranda sat back in her chair. "Never mind, Aud. I just don't like seeing you so upset. If you're so miserable, you should at least print the story you wrote and get something from the experience."

Audrey let the subject of Miranda's boyfriend go for now. She nodded, thinking about what she'd written. "I should apologize." She straightened in her chair. "I wonder if he'd see it...." she mumbled. She'd send a copy to John and Helen.

"What?" Claire asked.

"The story of how I deceived a good man," she answered, warming to the idea. It beat lying around feeling sorry for herself.

Mr. Burke might just go for a story about her experience undercover.

Miranda protested, "Audrey, you don't have to do that. Don't humiliate yourself that way."

Much as she appreciated Randa's concern, her sister didn't understand. This was not a pathetic attempt to gain a man's attention. "I'm not doing it for him. I'm doing it for me. I need to regain my honor. I was so desperate for...I don't know, something significant in my life, I convinced myself that the end justified the means." For the first time in two weeks, Audrey smiled, feeling a paradigm shift in her self-esteem. "I'm going to do what I should have done all along." She swallowed a bite of frozen yogurt. "Be myself."

When Audrey talked to Mr. Burke the next day, he gladly agreed. As a publicity stunt, it couldn't be beat.

The following week, Audrey hunched over her laptop around the clock. If she hadn't been writing on a PC, her bedroom would have been filled with thousands of crumpled pieces of paper. Considering she aspired to be a writer, one would think a story this personal would be child's play. But every attempt was deleted. Somehow, the words didn't sound right. They just weren't magic enough to convey her feelings.

Maybe mere words couldn't. Maybe she needed action.

"You seen this month's copy of *Dallas Today?*" John shoved the magazine under Mark's nose.

Mark was eating cold soup from a can while he watched the late news. It was after ten, and he'd just gotten in from the barn, where he'd been checking tack.

How many weeks, or months even, would it take for him to forget her? In every room in the house, Mark saw her. He woke in the middle of the night hot and hard, missing Audrey's soft breasts cushioning his head, aching for her touch—if he managed to sleep at all. He lay for hours envisioning the love in her eyes and the heat in her kisses. How could she have faked that kind of passion? It had felt so real, so strong.

What he should do was find another woman. A brunette. Maybe then he could forget.

His mood reflected the lack of sleep, and the hours of frustration. He impatiently barked out orders, working later and later each day. He knew he'd put off seeing his mom. He should've gone weeks ago, but just thinking about it made his stomach ache. He shoved the magazine back without looking. "How bad is it?"

"Oh, I think you'll wanna read this for yourself." John tossed the magazine in Mark's lap.

Well, damn. Had he really hoped she might have a scrap of principle? He should've been surprised it'd taken this long for the story to come out.

Mark forced his eyes open and read the caption: *Big Brothers to Benefit from Reporter's Blunder.*

"What the hell? What is this, John?"

John had a smug smirk on his face. "Read it."

"This would-be journalist made a horrible mistake. To get the scoop on a reclusive rodeo legend, I posed as a housekeeper on his ranch, the Double M.

I thought I'd meet a legend, write his story and ride off into the sunset. But Mark Malone is more than just a handsome cowboy with a bunch of gold buckles.

For two weeks, I had the privilege of getting to know the real *Lone Cowboy.* He's an honorable, generous man who's overcome obstacles that would make most men give up. But I was there under false pretenses and I regret betraying his trust.

As a gesture of my sincerity, I will be helping to raise money for Big Brothers and Big Sisters of America, the association Mark Malone spent so much of his time and money sponsoring over the years.

A fund-raiser will be held next Saturday, and I, personally, will be sitting on the platform at the dunking booth. So, come help a worthy cause...."

The article went on to give information on the date, place and time of the benefit.

Mark sat in stunned silence, disgusted with himself because all he could do at first was picture Audrey in a wet T-shirt, her nipples hard from the cold water. He was gonna need another cold shower tonight. "Damn it, she probably planned it that way."

"Of course she did. The question is, what are you going do about it?"

Mark jerked his gaze to John. "Nothing! She's not going to make a fool of me twice."

"Fool? She's tryin' to apologize."

Mark frowned at the magazine in his lap. "She's probably hoping I'll show up so she can have another story."

"You *are* a fool if you think that. She told Helen right before Keith came that she'd decided not to write a story about you, even if it meant losing her job."

Mark stood, ignoring the spark of hope those words had ignited and concentrating on John's betrayal. "You knew who she was? Why didn't you tell me?"

"Don't get your balls in a brace. Helen just told me last week. She thought it best not to interfere. She hoped, in time— Well, it doesn't matter now."

"I can understand how Audrey had you two suckered. It's myself I'm disgusted with. I knew better than to believe any woman could lo—" He stopped.

John finished his sentence. "Could love you? Don't you think it's possible she really does?"

Mark remembered Audrey whispering her love for him that first time, boldly proclaiming it the next. His chest constricted, and fury welled up in him.

He fought to keep his features blank. "I can do without her kind of love."

"Not all women are like your mother, Mark," John persisted.

Mark looked at the floor and hooked his thumbs in his pockets. "Maybe."

John folded his arms across his chest. "You've survived bulls and broncs, broken bones, a busted leg and booze. Don't you think you could handle the love of a good woman?"

Mark snorted. "There's no such thing. Not nowadays."

Fifteen

The drab little house on the north side of Fort Worth was even shabbier than Mark remembered. Keith had offered to go with him, but this was something he needed to do alone.

He parked his truck across the street and sat there for almost an hour, contemplating what he was about to do. He gripped the steering wheel like a lifeline, praying for the strength to get through this meeting with his mother.

She opened the door after the first knock—as if she'd been expecting someone. Her face was heavily made up, but he could still see the deep lines around her mouth, drooping bags under her eyes and sallow skin that declared a life of hard living. Her pantsuit was skintight on her still slim but sagging body, and she wore the same type of large, dangling earrings and bleached-blond hairdo he remembered from his childhood.

"If you're lookin' for Dudley, he ain't here," she snapped, a lit cigarette hanging from her bright red lips.

Mark swallowed hard. "Hello, Mama."

She leaned forward, squinted and peered closely for a few seconds. With her first and middle finger, she grabbed the cigarette from her mouth, leaned that same hand in the doorway and smiled, revealing yellowed smoker's teeth.

"I knew you'd come crawling back someday."

Mark's jaw hardened, his hands in tight fists at his side. "Can I come in?"

"Sure, sure. Come on in." She led him back to the small, dirty kitchen, waved him to a chair and grabbed two beer bottles from the fridge. Setting one on the table in front of him, she stubbed out her cigarette and said, "Sit down and have a cold one."

Mark took off his hat and sat down. He moved the beer away and put his hat on the table in front of him. The stench of stale beer, cigarettes and cheap perfume flooded his senses and unearthed long-repressed childhood memories. His throat was as dry as trail dust, and he couldn't seem to force any words past his lips.

"So? Whaddaya want? You ain't cuttin' me off, are ya? 'Cause I need that money." She plopped in a chair and lit another cigarette.

"No. You'll still get your money."

"Well? What is it then? Keith send you over here?" she sneered, and took a drag on her cigarette.

A small smile curved his lips. "In a way."

"Well, you can just tell him to keep his damn psycho-babble to himself! Thinks he's better than everybody 'cause he's getting some fancy-ass degree!" She took another drag.

Keith had warned him, but still, Mark shook his head in disgust. "You oughta feel lucky somebody cares enough to worry about you! Don't you ever think about anybody but yourself?"

She jumped from her chair and leaned across the table, hand raised, ready to strike. "Don't you talk to me that way, boy. I'm still your mother!"

Mark remembered when fear of her temper would make him stiffen in terror. But he'd learned to hide that terror with the same mask of indifference he hoped he displayed right now. He didn't move a muscle except to narrow his eyes. He wasn't scared, he wasn't even angry anymore. All he felt was a profound pity. What had Audrey said? *What a waste of a life.*

Like lightning in a summer storm, the truth hit him. It wasn't his fault. Audrey was right. He'd just been a young kid whose mother beat the crap out of him until one night he'd had enough. At ten years old, he couldn't have predicted the horrible consequences of his actions.

All these years he'd believed if he'd been smarter, or stronger, or worked harder, his parents wouldn't have gotten mad, would have loved him and Keith. If he hadn't told on his mom, they could have been a real family. But he saw now, it didn't matter.

It was like he'd been walking through life carrying a saddle on each shoulder. And now he tossed them off. He was free and the past no longer had power over him.

When she got no reaction from him, his mother sat down, breathing heavily and trembling, wariness in her eyes. "Dudley's gonna be home any minute! You better get out of here."

Mark leaned back. "I came to ask a favor. Some reporters might show up, askin' about me. I don't want you talkin' to 'em."

Her eyes widened in surprise. "Reporters? I don't

know," she said slyly. "What if they make me an offer I can't refuse?"

Mark took the hint. "How much?"

She smiled. "A couple of thousand oughta do me."

Mark slid his wallet from his back pocket and pulled out two hundred-dollar bills. "Here's a down payment. I'll have my business manager write you a check for the rest. If they offer you more, I'll double it."

She sneered and stubbed out her cigarette. "Think you can buy whatever you want now that you're so famous and all?"

Mark smiled sadly. He'd been wrong all these years. He'd been wrong about Audrey, too.

"What I needed, I got for free." He grabbed his hat and headed for his truck.

Audrey dipped her fingers in the tank of cold water, and a chill shot up her spine. She stood behind the dunking booth, tugging down the hem of the oversize Big Brothers T-shirt that covered her from neck to knees—for now, at least.

Underneath she wore only her one-piece swimsuit. It helped that her father and Miranda were there to show their support, but all she could think about was that once the T-shirt was off and the suit was wet, she might as well be naked.

All they needed was a patron to hand over his five dollars for three baseballs. Audrey was going to throw up. Her palms were sweaty, and her heart pounded in her chest.

But she had no regrets. Though she was nervous, she was also proud. A few months ago, she would never have been able to do something like this. Being with Mark might have cost her heart, but she was a stronger person for it. He'd seen her body and thought her beautiful, desirable. Never again would she sit on the sidelines while life passed her by. She had taken control.

Grudgingly, she acknowledged the irony of her situation. She hadn't taken a test yet, but she suspected she might be pregnant. She'd wanted to change her life, and that goal had certainly been accomplished.

Though she had moments of sheer terror, the thought of having a little chestnut-haired, blue-eyed boy or girl thrilled her. What would it be like to have a new life growing inside her?

"Hey, Toby! Here's that magazine woman. Let's dunk her!" The teenager, in baggy jeans and backward cap, handed the attendant five dollars and reached for his first baseball.

She reluctantly took off her T-shirt and stepped onto the dunking platform, shivering more from the humiliation of being so exposed than from the fear of being dunked.

"Aim good, Kyle!" the other teenager called.

"Piece of cake." The boy named Kyle raised his arm behind him.

Audrey squeezed her eyes shut. *This is a mistake. I can't do this. Everyone's staring at me!*

She heard a loud bang, but she didn't fall.

He'd missed! But he still had two more tries.

Another bang, another miss. This was too good to be true. Dare she hope?

"Hold it, son."

Audrey's eyes flew open. She froze like a marble statue, unable to speak or even breathe. He'd come. The black hat, the white shirt, the tight Wranglers. He looked like her hero from long ago.

"I'll donate five thousand dollars for a kiss from the lady."

Only now he was her tormentor.

The volunteer attendant whipped around to look at her, eyebrows raised, questioning. He did a double take at Mark. "Wait a minute. You're the *Lone Cowboy!* Can I have your autograph?"

Her father and Miranda shoved past the attendant, attempting to talk Mark out of his outrageous offer. Guess they thought she'd been humiliated enough. Both had the tempers to match their red hair. Miranda poked Mark in the chest, and her father raised his voice. Mark only stared at her saying nothing. The attendant and Kyle were yelling, and more people crowded around to see what the commotion was about.

Chaos ensued.

It was as if Audrey had been transported into some bizarre TV sitcom with no script. Fed up, she put her pinky fingers on either side of her mouth and whistled.

Instantly, silence reigned.

Audrey glared at Mark and climbed down from the platform. If he wanted a little extra revenge, so be it. She held his gaze as she approached. "Let's see the five thousand."

Mark reached into his jeans pocket, pulled out a wad of bills and slammed them on the booth's table. "Now, for my kiss."

Audrey scowled. Why was he doing this? Who cared? She threw her arms around his neck and smothered his mouth with hers.

Mark started to kiss her back, but pulled away, looking surprised.

Hah! She glared back at him. Did he think she'd cower and simper like a scared virgin? She wasn't that timid girl anymore. And she was through playing games. "I thought you wanted a kiss."

He stared at her a moment until a slow smile curved his lips. Then he took her face in his hands, bent close and kissed her back, long and deep.

Audrey heated and tingled under his sensual assault. His lips were firm and warm, and she drank him in like a tall glass of cool water after a day in the hot sun.

She opened her eyes when Mark slipped a hand under her knees and swung her up into his arms. She clutched his neck. "What are you doing?" she hissed.

"You're through for the day," he answered, his voice raspy. "The dunking booth made its quota." He headed toward the outer doors.

"Put me down." She wiggled and pushed against him, but he held her in an iron grip.

"For crying out loud. You're not heavy!"

"I didn't say I was. But I'm not—" she smacked his chest and continued fighting "—going with you."

Mark squeezed her closer and narrowed his eyes. "Yes, you are. Now quit squirmin'."

She stilled. The heat from his body inflamed her. She was tempted to run her hands down his muscled arms and up to his broad shoulders. But she forced herself to look at him. "Where are we going?"

Mark lowered his gaze to her chest. His jaw clenched and his eyes narrowed. "Cover up, or I won't be responsible for my actions." He gestured with his head to her T-shirt he'd picked up along the way.

Of all the nerve! She didn't know which to respond to first, being kidnapped or being ridiculed. But she gratefully grabbed the shirt off his shoulder and draped it across her chest.

Mark stepped through the outer door of the Dallas Convention Center, stopped and turned around. "Smile and wave at your dad. Tell him you're fine and you'll see him later."

"But where are we going?"

"Just do it, damn it!"

Audrey reluctantly did as he bid.

At least her dad had quit following them, and even smiled at her. She caught a glimpse of John leading him away.

Mark whisked her into a waiting limo, maneuvered himself in beside her and the chauffeur took off. Snatching off his hat, Mark tossed it on the opposite seat and ran a hand through his hair. He didn't speak or look at her.

His hair was a little longer, and dark circles shadowed his eyes. But he was clean shaven, and smelled of his unique musky scent. His arm held her tight against him.

She swallowed past the lump in her throat. "So? What do you want?"

Mark turned to her, and she thought she glimpsed a flicker of passion in his eyes. But the next moment it was gone. What more could he want? Audrey raised her arms and began putting her head through the T-shirt's neck opening.

Mark reached over and stopped her.

"I thought you wanted me to cover up?"

His eyes swept over her breasts and he took a deep breath. "Changed my mind."

She twisted away from his grasp and continued dressing, daring him to stop her. Just because she felt badly about deceiving him didn't mean she'd revert to being a doormat.

Though she struggled, Mark easily wrenched the shirt from her hands. He grabbed her wrists, held them over her head and pushed her down to the plush leather seat.

The full weight of his body pressed her down, his

breathing as ragged as hers. She looked into his oh-so-beautiful blue eyes, striving for composure, determined not to let him guess she was aroused.

"Look, I know I lied to you. But I never printed your secrets, and I apologized publicly. What more do you want? Isn't this taking things a bit far?"

"Not far enough, darlin'." He captured her lips with his, kissing her until she whimpered.

She wished he'd let go of her hands so she could run them through his hair and reacquaint herself with the feel of him. She soon got her wish, but he only released one.

His free hand glided down her hair to her shoulder, lowering her suit strap and landing firmly on her breast to squeeze and caress.

If he meant to punish her, he was succeeding. She ached for him. "Let me up."

He ignored her plea, kissing down the line of her throat.

She pushed against his shoulder with her free hand. "Please. Don't do this."

"Why not?" he grumbled, lifting his head to look at her with narrowed eyes. "Didn't you mean what you said in the field that night?"

She bit back the resounding "yes" on the tip of her tongue. Was he serious, or playing some cruel game? Maybe it would be better to let him think she'd lied. He already had several advantages in this situation—her guilt and his strength. Why give him one more? Besides, the last thing she needed was more humiliation or pity.

Mark let out a sigh. Was that disappointment she'd seen in his face before he'd shuttered his expression? "All right. Guess we'll do this the hard way." Slowly, he let her go and sat up.

Audrey scooted away, sat up and pulled her bathing suit

strap over her shoulder. She gathered the T-shirt in front of her. "What do you want?"

Mark slid close and put his arm across the back of the seat. He turned to her and grinned. "One more high-stakes game, darlin'."

The force of that gorgeous smile hit her like a windstorm, chasing away her caution. High stakes? For a moment, she envisioned wedding bells and happy ever after.

If only.

He was so handsome it made her stomach clench. But that only strengthened her belief that he was way beyond her reach. He was limousines and private jets, beauty queens and television ads.

She was hatchbacks, plus sizes and macaroni and cheese.

She had three choices. She could bluff her way out— threaten to press charges and demand to be let go. But he'd probably call her bluff. Or she could plead for leniency. Or she could simply wait, and face her fate with what dignity she had left.

She chose dignity.

She looked away, out the tinted window. "Fine. Let's get it over with."

His fingers caught her chin, forcing her to turn toward him. No longer smiling, his eyes burned into her. "It'll be a long time before it's over, darlin'."

Abruptly, he leaned forward and tapped on the glass. The chauffeur lowered the barrier. "Yes, sir?"

"Where's the deck of cards in this thing?"

"In the right side compartment, sir."

"Thank you."

As the glass rose, Audrey racked her brain to guess his intentions. He wanted to play poker now?

He reached over her to grab the cards, and she scooted a little farther away, clutching the T-shirt like a shield. If only she had her clothes on, she wouldn't feel quite so vulnerable.

"One game." He shuffled the cards. "You cut. I'll deal. Five-card draw, nothing wild, winner takes all." He placed the deck on the seat between them. "Cut."

To Audrey, the deck might as well have been a rattler about to strike. "But, I don't have any money with me. What are the stakes?"

"Stakes?" Mark smiled again—a dangerous smile. "I told you. The stakes are high, darlin'."

Sixteen

A surge of triumph filled Mark's chest. Her eyes widened, and she gripped that damn shirt as if it was the only thing standing between her and complete ravishment.

Maybe she was right.

He couldn't take his eyes off of her. A deep pink flush spread down her cheeks. Her hair was twisted on top of her head, a few curly tendrils hanging around her face. She was beautiful. When she'd planted that kiss on him, her back ramrod straight and her green eyes sparked with challenge, the blood had rushed to his groin so fast he'd actually felt light-headed.

He had to remind himself to stay focused on the plan. Hiring that kid to throw and miss had been sheer inspiration. But it was a good thing the traffic on I-30 was bumper-to-bumper from Dallas to Fort Worth. She was being stubborn. Or did she really not love him? He'd never understand women. That night in the meadow, he couldn't keep her from saying she loved him. Now, he needed to hear her admit it. Only the fire in her sea-green eyes gave him hope.

"S-so, what are these high stakes?" Her voice trembled.

He wanted to hold her and tell her it would be all right. And he would...eventually. "Come on, Audrey. Show your sack." He flashed her the same evil grin she'd given him.

She played right into his hands. Gone was the cowering girl, and in her place was the strong woman he admired. Her spine straightened, and her chin came up. She even dropped the shirt.

"All right. I assume you had something in mind? You want my job? I'll quit, but I'm a good writer. I'll find something else. You want sex? I don't see why. You said you'd gotten what you want—"

"Hold it!" Mark said. "Let's get one thing straight right now. That was never the—" *Spit it out, Malone.* "Aw, hell, Audrey. You know it was good. Better than good."

She became intensely interested in the limo's upholstery. But at least he'd shut her up. "Now, as to the stakes. We'll play one game. If you win, you get the Double M."

"Your ranch?" Audrey gripped his arm. "You can't do that! I haven't got anything that valuable."

The way she leaned over afforded him a fantastic view of two very valuable assets. But he didn't think she'd appreciate his sentiments. He forced his gaze to her eyes. "The Double M is worthless without you there, Audrey." It was true. He'd sell the place if he couldn't have her with him.

She shook her head. "Me? But you hate me. I lied to you."

If she only knew how much he loved her. But he had to know she really loved him first. "If I win, I get you. In the limo. Right now. Without the suit."

"Here? But, everyone can see in. What about the driver?"

"He can't see anything. It's one-way glass. All the windows are."

For once, Mark couldn't tell what thoughts were whirling around in Audrey's usually expressive face. Finally, she took a deep breath and said, "All right. But I can't take your ranch. I just want to hear you say you forgive me."

"Done." It didn't matter what he bet. Either way, he won.

Mark dealt them each five cards.

As Audrey picked hers up, it took all her self-control not to smile. Eight of hearts, seven of hearts, six of hearts, five of hearts and a three of clubs. What were the odds? Was he dealing straight or was this a setup?

No way. Besides, why go to all this trouble?

He caught her studying him and grinned. "Cards?"

She looked him in the eye but kept her face unreadable. "One, please." She slid her three of clubs over the seat.

The smug curve of his lips said he wasn't impressed as he dealt her one card. "Dealer takes one, also." His face remained blank as he looked at his new card.

Audrey steeled herself to remain expressionless as she glanced quickly at her new card. She almost gave it away when she saw the four of hearts. A straight flush! No way could he possibly beat that. It would be too unbelievable. She'd won! Oh, it was hard not to grin triumphantly. "Well, Mr. Malone. What've you got?"

Without hesitation, Mark laid down his hand: three aces and two jacks. A full house. Normally a winning hand.

She pictured his face when she showed him her cards, imagined hearing his grudging words of forgiveness. But just because he said the words didn't mean that, deep in his heart, he had actually forgiven her.

It would be an empty victory. A sham. No bet could give her what she really wanted—his love.

Maybe if she lost and he got his revenge, he would at least be free to get on with his life. What was a little humiliation compared to that? She knew he wouldn't hurt her. She loved him. She wanted him happy. If that's what it took, that's what she'd do.

With her decision made, her worries vanished. Might as well enjoy this last time with him. One more memory for those lonely nights.

She reached for her window button and lowered the glass a few inches. Holding his gaze, she lifted her arm behind her and let her cards fly out the window. She raised the window and brought her hand to the strap of her bathing suit, lowering it slowly. "You win." She smiled.

Mark sat there a moment, stunned at the realization that she was finally his. Well, that and the fact that she smiled as if *she* was the one who had won as she willingly stripped off her bathing suit.

She pulled out one arm and lowered the other strap. Mark swallowed, twice.

Last time, he'd refused to make love with her on a bet. But that was before she'd told him she loved him. The stakes were too high now. She must love him if she could smile that way as she gradually lowered the suit to her waist. Her nipples were already tight and pointed, begging for his mouth. He licked his lips in anticipation. He wanted his mouth on her now, but he forced himself to wait and enjoy the show she so freely offered. Besides, there was one more thing to do first.

She briefly glanced at the driver, and for a split second Mark saw her confidence slip, but she quickly masked her uncertainty. What a woman.

And from this moment on, she was all his.

Audrey couldn't believe she was doing this. Kind of hard to remove a bathing suit seductively in the seat of a car, even if it was a limousine. Well, maybe some women could do it, but not her.

Still, faster than she wished, here she sat in all her naked, chubby glory. She kept her arms at her sides and boldly dared him to look his fill.

His eyes roamed over her body, leisurely exploring her from top to bottom with obvious approval. Not knowing what to expect, she flinched when he began unbuttoning his shirt.

His chest muscles rippled as he pulled his sleeves off and threw the shirt on the floor. She caught a whiff of masculine sweat and musky cologne, and breathed in deeply.

He unbuckled his belt and unzipped his jeans. As he watched her watching him, he pushed his jeans down, taking his briefs with them until he reached his boots. He swung his legs onto her lap, silently asking her to tug off his boots and jeans.

Dazed, she complied, her eyes roving from his strong, hairy chest, to his flat stomach, to his long, muscular thighs and finally coming to rest on his potent male organ.

Enthralled with his nakedness, she jumped when he finally spoke. "You're the only woman besides hospital nurses who's seen me like this." He narrowed his eyes and jerked his chin at his leg. "Take a good look, Audrey. Disgusting, isn't it?"

She looked.

Where the left leg had a light dusting of brown hair, the right was covered only in scars. In addition to the long, thick one that snaked around from thigh to ankle, there were dozens of tiny white scars scattered around. The knee was sunken and the calf malformed. It wasn't a pretty sight. To her, it was a miracle he could walk at all, much less ride. Thinking of his persistence and determination to recover overwhelmed her.

She met his eyes. If he was anxious about her opinion, he didn't show it. Looking down, she ran her hand over his leg as she spoke. "I think it's a miracle. A testament to your strength and your indomitable will."

When he grabbed her hand and squeezed it, she raised her gaze to his again. She hoped he could read the truth of her heart in her eyes.

His were filled with unshed tears, brimming over, threatening to spill down his cheeks. He pushed her down, taking full possession of her mouth. After kissing her senseless, he pulled away and scowled. "Why did you lie to me, Audrey?"

This isn't exactly how she'd pictured herself explaining to him. She only hoped she could make him understand. "I spent my twenty-fifth birthday alone." She laughed, a short, humorless sound. "I don't even have a dog. I thought a more challenging career would fill the emptiness in my life. I needed something more."

He brushed his lips over her eyes, cheeks and forehead. "But you gave that up, lost your promotion, for me?"

"Once I got to know you, I couldn't betray your trust. Not even for the good of my career. I wouldn't have been able to face myself in the mirror. Besides, I got my promotion. I'm going to write more articles on charity events like this one."

He ran his hands through her hair, down her throat, over her breast and stomach. "And do you still need more?"

When she could breathe again, she answered, "Yes."

"What do you need?" He lifted himself over her, his magic fingers delving between her thighs.

This, she thought, closing her eyes. Oh yes, this. And so much more. "I—I need for you to understand, and to forgive me."

His fingers dug into her arms and she opened her eyes. He looked menacing. "Don't ever lie to me again."

She shook her head. "Never."

"Okay." He smiled. "Then, I forgive you."

She threw her arms around his neck and hugged him. "Thank you."

"After you left, I almost started drinking again. I hated you."

Audrey held her breath. She couldn't live knowing he despised her. "But, you don't anymore?"

"John told me you confessed to Helen. And even if you'd lied about who you were, you couldn't have faked it all. Your passion, your belief in me, not as the *Lone Cowboy,* but as Mark, just plain Mark. You made me believe in myself." He opened his mouth over hers and kissed her again. "Was it just an act?"

Hadn't he heard anything she'd said? Didn't he know? She lifted her head to return his kiss.

He took control of the kiss, plunging in his tongue. Abruptly, he pulled back. "Say it, Audrey. Tell me."

She had no reason not to tell him now. "I love you, Mark."

"Yes." He growled the word as he entered her, and said it again and again as he moved in her. He took her hard and swift, and they both spiraled swiftly to completion.

She could feel his heart racing even when he raised himself on his elbows and put his palm on her cheek, forcing her to look at him. "Say it again."

"I love you, Mark."

He smiled. "I want to hear you say it every day. And I don't want you doin' all the cleanin' and cookin' anymore. We'll hire someone to help."

"Wait a minute."

"Especially if you get pregnant. We can have the wedding here in Fort Worth if you want. I figure you'll want your family—"

She put her hand over his mouth. "Mark! What are you talking about?"

He looked at her as if she were a little slow. "Us. The ranch. Everything."

"You want me to live at the ranch?"

"You want to live in Dallas? I guess we can buy a house here. But I need to be on the Double M most of the time."

"But—"

"What? You're worried about your career? I'm sure you could still write for the magazine, but I kinda hoped you'd wanna stay home with the babies, too."

"Mark." She shook his shoulders. "What babies?"

Now he looked exasperated. "Our babies. The ones we're gonna have some day. Maybe you could work from home. We—"

She smacked her hand over his mouth again, but took it away before she spoke. "Did you mention the word wedding?"

"Yeah."

"But you haven't asked me."

"Woman, you're gonna marry me—"

"I'd like to be asked." She smiled.

Mark narrowed his eyes and let out a long, suffering sigh. "Ms. Tyson, would you do me the honor of becoming my wife?"

"No."

"What? Why not? You said you loved me."

Audrey looked away. Would she have to force him to say it? "But you haven't," she barely whispered.

Mark broke into a wide grin. "I love you, Audrey. I love your beautiful eyes, your smile, your—" he squeezed her breast "—your spirit. Now, are you going to marry me, or do you want to be dragged back to the Double M to live in sin?"

Oh, how she loved hearing those four words. She knew she would never feel empty again. Still, she hesitated. One more thing should be discussed.

As she thought about how to tell him, his grin faded into a mask of indifference. "If you really don't want to marry me…." he whispered.

Oh, she'd hesitated too long. "No! That's not it at all. It's just that—" Should she tell him when she wasn't sure? "Our first baby might be here in about eight months."

His eyes widened and his whole body went rigid, but he remained silent.

"Mark? Do you understand? Are you upset?"

A slow smile spread across his face. "Upset, darlin'? How could I be upset?" He wrapped his arms beneath her and squeezed her to him. "I'm gonna be the best damn father, I swear!"

"I know you will. And, if you're sure, I'll marry you."

"You bet you're gonna marry me, woman, if I have to lasso you and tie you to a church pew."

Audrey giggled. "I think we've had enough bets for a while. Would you really have given me the ranch if I'd won?"

"Honey, no stakes are too high for you." Mark grinned. He swooped down for another kiss.

Audrey whispered against his lips, "As long as the stakes are love, Mark."

Epilogue

Cowboy Christmas. The Fourth of July weekend had taken on a whole new meaning.

This year, instead of traveling from city to city, riding in two or sometimes three rodeos for prize money, Mark was flipping burgers on a backyard grill and watching his four-month-old daughter play in her bouncy chair on the porch. Alyse Helen Malone had her daddy's blue eyes and her mama's blond hair.

Mark gazed around the yard that had changed almost as much as its owner. Instead of choking weeds and a scum-laden pool, the back of his house now hosted the first annual Big Brothers and Big Sisters Dude Ranch Weekend. Dozens of fatherless boys and girls ran around playing baseball, squirting water guns, riding ponies and splashing in the pool.

"Is she doing okay?" his wife called as she shouldered her way out the back door carrying a large bowl of chips.

His wife. He still couldn't believe he'd found this kind of love. Though, last month they'd celebrated their first wedding anniversary.

"My little angel?" Mark smiled as he set down the spatula and picked up his daughter. He brought his forefinger to Alyse's nose and wiggled it. She gave him a grin, showing off her first tooth.

"Angel! Little hellion is more like it." Audrey smiled at her baby girl, belying her words. Audrey looked around the yard. "I never would have thought I'd end up married to the *Lone Cowboy.*" She looked at him with the same wonder and joy in her eyes that he imagined showed in his.

Audrey put a hand on his shoulder and bounced up on her tiptoes to give him a kiss. "Thank you, Mr. Malone."

Just her touch had the power to undo him. Mark swallowed the lump in his throat. He couldn't afford to get all mushy in front of these kids. But, wait until tonight. "You don't have to thank me. I love having the kids here. It was a great idea, Audrey."

"Not for this. For trusting me with your heart after what I did."

Mark raised Alyse onto his shoulder. "Oh, that. Well, it was just a scarred, shriveled up lump of horse dung before you came along. I'd take that ride again in a heartbeat, darlin'. The best ride of my life. I fell hard and landed right in your arms." He grinned and bent to kiss her beautiful lips, smiling down at her emerald eyes.

Oh, what the hell. Who cared whether he had an audience. He gently set Alyse in her carrier and swept Audrey into his arms. Bending her backward, he closed his lips over hers, pouring all his passion and promise for tonight into his kiss.

* * * * *

DYNASTIES: THE ASHTONS

**A family built on lies...
brought together by dark,
passionate secrets.**

JUST A TASTE

(Silhouette Desire #1645,
available April 2005)

by Bronwyn Jameson

When Jillian Ashton's arrogant
husband died, it wasn't long before
she found a man who treated her
right—*really* right. Problem was,
Seth—a tall, dark and handsome
hunk—was her late husband's
brother. She'd planned on just
a taste of his tender touch, but
was left wanting more....

*Available at your
favorite retail outlet.*

presents

BEYOND BUSINESS

(SD #1649, April 2005)

by Rochelle Alers

The sizzling conclusion of

THE BLACKSTONES OF VIRGINIA

Seduction is on the agenda for patriarch
Sheldon Blackstone when he learns his new secretary
is sexy *and* expecting! A widower who never thought
he'd have a second chance at love, Sheldon must
convince the commitment-wary career woman to
trust her heart and begin a new family with him on
his sprawling, glamorous plantation.

Available at your favorite retail outlet.

HARLEQUIN® *Blaze*™

Get ready to check in to Hush…

Piper Devon has opened a hot new hotel
that caters to the senses…and it's giving
ex-lover Trace Winslow a few sleepless nights.

Check out

#178 HUSH

by Jo Leigh

Available April 2005

Book #1, Do Not Disturb miniseries

Look for linked stories by Isabel Sharpe,
Alison Kent, Nancy Warren, Debbi Rawlins
and Jill Shalvis in the months to come!

Shhh…Do Not Disturb

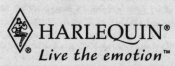

HARLEQUIN®
Live the emotion™

If you enjoyed what you just read,
then we've got an offer you can't resist!

Take 2 bestselling
love stories FREE!
Plus get a FREE surprise gift!

COMING NEXT MONTH

#1645 JUST A TASTE—Bronwyn Jameson
Dynasties: The Ashtons
When Jillian Ashton's arrogant husband died, it wasn't long before she found a man who treated her right—*really* right. Problem was, Seth—a tall, dark and handsome hunk—was her late husband's brother. She'd planned on just a taste of his tender touch, but was left wanting more....

#1646 DOUBLE IDENTITY—Annette Broadrick
The Crenshaws of Texas
Undercover agent Jude Crenshaw only meant to attract Carina Patterson for the sake of cracking a case against her brothers. But when close quarters turned his business into their pleasure, Jude could only hope his double identity wouldn't turn their new union into two broken hearts.

#1647 RULES OF ATTRACTION—Susan Crosby
Behind Closed Doors
P.I. Quinn Gerard was following a suspected accomplice—or so he thought. When the sexy bombshell turned out to be her twin sister, Claire, Quinn no longer had to watch her every move. But he couldn't seem to take his eyes off her! Could Quinn convince Claire to bend the rules and give in to their mutual attraction?

#1648 WHEN THE EARTH MOVES—Roxanne St. Claire
After Jo Ellen Tremaine's best friend died during an earthquake, she was determined to adopt her friend's baby girl. But first she needed the permission of the girl's stunningly sexy uncle—big-shot attorney Cameron McGrath. Cameron always had a weakness for wildly attractive women, but neither was prepared for the aftershocks of this seismic shift....

#1649 BEYOND BUSINESS—Rochelle Alers
The Blackstones of Virginia
Blackstone Farms owner Sheldon Blackstone couldn't help but be enraptured by his newly hired assistant, Renee Williams. Little did he know she was pregnant with her ex's baby. Renee was totally taken by this older man, but could she convince him to make her—and her child—his forever?

#1650 SLEEPING ARRANGEMENTS—Amy Jo Cousins
The terms of the will were clear: in order to gain her inheritance Addy Tyler needed to be married. Enter the one man she never dreamed would become her groom of convenience—Spencer Reed. Their marriage was supposed to be hands-off, but their sleeping arrangements changed everything!

SDCNM0305